The Worse Th̶
Was Knowing ̶
Rest Of The Day…
And Night…Alone With Annie.

She got under his skin and he didn't like it one bit.
He was a one-woman man and his woman had been
violently taken from him. Other women, no matter
how inviting, were distractions he just didn't need.

He needed to remain frozen and apart. Distance let
him maintain his emotional balance. Cold hearts
didn't feel guilt. Being numb meant keeping the
pain at bay.

Nick had spent two long years keeping his distance
from life, and damned if Annie didn't bring that
tempting heat right on to the island with her.

Heat and wanting.

Dear Reader,

Welcome to another fabulous month of novels from Silhouette Desire. Our DYNASTIES: THE ASHTONS continuity continues with Kristi Gold's *Mistaken for a Mistress*. Ford Ashton sets out to find the truth about who really murdered his grandfather and believes the answers may lie with the man's mistress—but who is Kerry Roarke *really*? *USA TODAY* bestselling author Jennifer Greene is back with a stellar novel, *Hot to the Touch*. You'll love this wounded veteran hero and the feisty female whose special touch heals him.

TEXAS CATTLEMAN'S CLUB: THE SECRET DIARY presents its second installment with *Less-than-Innocent Invitation* by Shirley Rogers. It seems this millionaire rancher has to keep tabs on his ex-girlfriend by putting her up at his Texas spread. Oh, poor girl…trapped with a sexy—wealthy— cowboy! There's a brand-new KING OF HEARTS book by Katherine Garbera as the mysterious El Rey's matchmaking attempts continue in *Rock Me All Night*. Linda Conrad begins a compelling new miniseries called THE GYPSY INHERITANCE, the first of which is *Seduction by the Book*. Look for the remaining two novels to follow in September and October. And finally, Laura Wright winds up her royal series with *Her Royal Bed*. There's lots of revenge, royalty and romance to be enjoyed.

Thanks for choosing Silhouette Desire. In the coming months be sure to look for titles by authors Peggy Moreland, Annette Broadrick and the incomparable Diana Palmer.

Happy reading!

Melissa Jeglinski

Melissa Jeglinski
Senior Editor
Silhouette Desire

Please address questions and book requests to:
Silhouette Reader Service
U.S.: 3010 Walden Ave., P.O. Box 1325, Buffalo, NY 14269
Canadian: P.O. Box 609, Fort Erie, Ont. L2A 5X3

SEDUCTION
BY THE BOOK
LINDA CONRAD

Silhouette Desire

Published by Silhouette Books

America's Publisher of Contemporary Romance

 **SILHOUETTE BOOKS**

ISBN 0-373-76673-4

SEDUCTION BY THE BOOK

Visit Silhouette Books at www.eHarlequin.com

Printed in U.S.A.

LINDA CONRAD

Award-winning author Linda Conrad was first inspired by her mother, who gave her a deep love of storytelling. "Actually, Mom told me I was the best liar she ever knew. And that's saying something for a woman with an Irish-storyteller's background," Linda says. In her past life Linda was a stockbroker and certified financial planner, but she has been writing contemporary romances for six years now. Linda's passions are her husband, her cat named Sam and finding time to read cozy mysteries and emotional love stories. She says, "Living with passion makes everything worthwhile." Visit Linda's Web site at www.LindaConrad.com or write to her at P.O. Box 9269, Tavernier, FL 33070.

For Captain Jeremy Steele-Perkins,
thanks for the long-distance sailing lessons!
If there are still mistakes in the terms, it's my fault!
And my most sincere appreciation to his wife,
my dear agent Pattie, for her ultimate assistance
with this Gypsy series. She knows why.

Also, a big thanks to the great women
at the e-Harlequin Desireables monthly chats, especially
Marilyn, Bren and Emilie for all their wonderful
suggestions of Gypsy titles. Thanks again, guys!

Prologue

The smells of French pastry, boiled crayfish and scented table candles filled the sultry air. Paper lanterns, laughing couples strolling wide sidewalks and twinkling lights all made for a merry party atmosphere.

But none of it made a difference to Passionata Chagari. It was her duty to be here in the French Quarter this evening. Her duty to fulfill her father's dying wishes.

She swung the multicolored shawl around her shoulders to protect against the crisp December night and looked down under the table to be sure the old treasure chest was safe and unseen. Her father, the late king of the gypsies, had left a chest full of bequests of magic to the young men of the prominent Steele family. Young men the king had never met. He had also directed Passionata from his grave to see the gifts delivered and used to their proper purpose.

And that she would do gladly. After all, she too owed much to the late Lucille Steele. So Lucille's blood descendants were about to receive a boon, in payment for the ultimate act of kindness.

From Passionata's position, sitting at the white-draped table with her crystal ball directly in front of her, she could see the approach of her current target—Nicholas Scoville, great nephew of Lucille—as he used a cane and limped in her direction.

A tall and quite handsome young man dressed in a dark gray European suit, Nicholas was strong of heart yet currently weak of body and soul. His old knee injury was acting up tonight, she knew. But what Passionata had in mind for him would eventually take away all his pain.

Passionata smiled to herself. This young descendent of Lucille Steele, who needed help so desperately, should be the easiest one to assist.

He wouldn't admit it readily, but deep in his soul Nicholas already believed in the power of magic. The passion of her father's legacy should be quite a relief to this young man who was so controlled by obligation and guilt.

She saw Nicholas in the distance as he leaned heavily on his walking stick and looked around the crowded square for someplace to wait. Passionata directed her thoughts toward bringing him closer.

With his attention turned elsewhere, Nicholas absently sat down at her table. She waited for him to become aware of her presence.

Finally, he turned to her with a start. "May I rest here a few minutes, old woman? I have an appointment and need to kill some time, but I don't need my fortune told."

"Welcome, Nicholas Scoville," she whispered. "I have been waiting for you."

"You must recognize me from photos of my great-aunt's funeral in the papers." He scowled at her. "But don't think you can con me just because you know my name. I only need a spot to rest for a few minutes. Nothing more."

She grinned with a knowing and sly smile. "You need a great deal more than that, young friend."

For example, later tonight she knew that he would be going in search of a personal trainer to work with him toward his knee's recovery. Passionata had already placed the *right* person in his path and the wheels of fate were set in motion. But that would only be the first step to his ultimate legacy.

"I have something to help you." She reached into the chest under the table and produced a book with a heavy, inlaid covering. "This is but one part of the legacy left to Lucille Steele's heirs. It has been bequeathed to you from my father in payment for a debt owed to her."

"Great-aunt Lucille? If you have something owed to her, you need to contact her estate attorneys."

"No," she argued. "This book is a special gift, made for you alone." Passionata shoved the journal-sized book toward him, and he automatically reached a hand out to take it from her.

Nicholas looked down at the original edition of *The Grimm Brothers' Children's and Household Tales* with its exquisite gold-and-ivory inlaid cover. She could see his fascination and curiosity grow.

"You must be mistaken," he said once again, without looking away from the book. "Perhaps someone in my mother's family is a first edition collector. But I am not."

"Look for your name burnished on the back, Nicholas Scoville. This book will lead you to accept your destiny. Accept it. Cherish it."

She watched him slowly turn the cover over in his hand before she silently took her leave. When he finally looked up with questions in his eyes, he found himself sitting all alone at the table.

But Passionata would be watching. Watching and waiting for her father's legacy to weave its magic for Nicholas Scoville.

One

Six months later

Some battles even the bravest, strongest human being on earth should not attempt.

Annie Riley sighed and held the phone away from her ear. Facing the wrath of her mother, Maeve Mary Margaret O'Brien Riley, even just on the telephone from all the way back home in South Boston, was one of those battles.

But her mother was over a thousand miles away, and Annie had grown up and become stronger in the past six months that she'd been away from home. She put the earpiece back to her ear and tried to interrupt the steady stream of half Gaelic, half English words, spoken with determined but soft and lilting tones.

"Ma, please listen," she begged. "I'll be perfectly

safe, staying on the island. The weatherman says the storm will probably miss us by fifty miles."

"Your brother, Michael, tells me that this hurricane is a hundred miles across and headed right in your direction."

Bless her older brother's devilish little Irish heart. So what if Michael worked at a television station and probably had access to good weather information. He was *so* not a weather forecaster. He'd only mentioned the storm's width to their mother in order to cause trouble.

She missed her family, but having so many older brothers and sisters was one of the very reasons Annie had decided she needed to leave home—leave South Boston—leave the entire continental United States.

"Does that boss of yours insist that you stay?" her mother demanded. "I'll bet he's already left, hasn't he?"

"No. As a matter of fact, Nick refuses to leave the island even though two of the research facility team leaders have volunteered to stay." Annie wouldn't tell her mother that she'd had a difficult time convincing Nick that she too should stay on the island. The man was just plain stubborn.

"Oh, I hadn't thought of those lovely fish. What will happen to them in the storm?"

"Not fish, Ma. Dolphins are mammals. They even breathe air, just like people do. And there's a big elaborate plan for what will happen to them in the storm." This conversation was getting her nowhere.

"Well, your boss *should* stay," her mother declared forcefully. "The Scoville family owns most of that island. But you're just an employee. You have nothing there to lose…but your life."

"Please don't be so melodramatic, Ma. I'll be fine. Caribbean islands come through hurricanes all the time with no problem. The islanders here have already boarded up everything for us, and I've put extra food, water and batteries in the big house's pantry. We're all set."

"Ah, *dervla*," her mother sighed, using the old Gaelic word for daughter. "Must you stay on that private island? You'll give your poor mother a heart attack with such worry."

Her mother was pulling out all the big guns now. Hide, Annie Riley, she warned herself. A thousand miles away wasn't far enough when her mother began her pity routine.

Annie took a deep breath and decided to try a different tactic altogether. "You have six other kids and nine grandchildren to worry about, Ma. Some of them have real problems. This is just a hurricane. You know no Riley would ever let a little storm stop them.

"By the way," she continued, sure her plan to distract her mother would work. "How is Da doing with his rehabilitation after the heart attack? It's been nearly a year. Is he sticking to it?"

The mention of her grandchildren and her husband's close call with death slowed down Maeve Riley's words. Annie knew she had won this battle by diversion, even though every member of her family was truly just fine. But she could never hope to win the war. Her mother would forever be overprotective of her baby daughter. Annie had accepted that fact long ago—and had finally found a way to leave home so she could live her own life.

As she listened with one ear to her mother go on about her loved ones not practicing the Irish good sense God gave them, Annie turned her thoughts to what she could do to best help the man she'd come to think of as a lost storybook prince—Nicholas Scoville, the man for whom she would gladly face a hurricane any day.

Annie stuck her head out of the one door left ajar and glanced hesitatingly up at the deep gray sky. It was a funny shade. Not the ugly black that the skies here sometimes became during a wild tropical thunderstorm.

No, this sky was the color of her father's Sunday suit, a kind of pigeon-gray. And huge beige clouds swirled so quickly past above where she stood that they made the whole heavens look as if some leprechaun had hit the fast forward button on a DVD player.

The storm must be getting closer. She would have to turn on the radio and check its position—just as soon as she checked her boss's position.

The last time she'd seen Nick he was headed down the beach toward the dolphin research and rehabilitation facility to check on the pod. But Annie was positive that the dolphins would be safe in their lagoon.

One of the team members who had volunteered to stay with them through the storm was a former Navy SEAL. The other was a woman who had scientific credentials from seven international universities. It was rumored she could talk to the dolphins in their own language.

Annie smiled at the thought. She liked the dolphins. The few times she'd been able to go down to the research center had been wonderful fun. The dolphins seemed happy to be playing with the handlers.

Easing out of the doorway, she almost lost her balance. The winds were so strong they nearly knocked her to the ground. She set her feet and held herself erect the same way she would've done back on the high school gymnastic team's balance beams.

She faced the wind and thought it was exhilarating, pitting herself against nature. The salty air and the roar of the winds and ocean made her feel so alive. The only problem Annie had with the winds now was keeping her unruly hair out of her eyes long enough to see where she was going.

She hadn't had the darn mass of curls trimmed for the whole six months she'd been Nick's personal trainer. This was as long as her hair had grown since she was ten—when her mother cut off her braids because she kept getting them caught in things. Things like the kitchen door as she was heading outside at a dead run.

As Annie made her way to the edge of the enormous patio, she held back her hair and squinted out toward the ocean. Moving her gaze past the shallow cliff where she stood, she searched the wide, white sand beach.

She saw him, standing on a spit of sand at the ocean's edge with his back to her. Nick faced into the wind as he stared out at the water.

Trying to call out to him, her voice was lost in the roaring winds. He needed to come back to the main house. The storm must be very close, and she had given her promise to his mother that she would watch out for him. She took that duty very seriously.

The longer she stayed in his employ, though, the stronger her reactions to the sight of him. As usual, today he was a solitary figure surveying his kingdom.

She flew down the steps to the beach and ran head-long into the wind to reach him. "Nick! Come inside now."

He must've heard her, or perhaps just sensed her presence, because he turned around. "What do you want? Dammit! You should be in the main house," he said tightly.

His voice was thunderous, his face distorted in a scowl. But he was still so handsome and such a mascu-line presence, standing there with his arms crossed over his chest, that her breath caught in her throat.

It was bad enough that he lived in an enchanted cas-tle, high on a cliff overlooking the ocean. But he'd al-ways reminded Annie of a bewitched fairy-tale figure, one who pinned away for a lost lover to come break the spell that he had been put under by an evil witch.

Except that this fairy-tale figure could sometimes be the most infuriating person on earth. He was aloof and demanding. She'd given him a lot of leeway when they'd first begun training because of his circum-stances and because she knew he was in pain.

But many times recently she had been ready to call it a day and walk out on him. At this point in his recov-ery he was nearly healed and his pains were nothing but echoes.

Only two things had kept her here on his island, put-ting up with his irritating manner. First was her prom-ise to his mother to try to bring him out of his shell. The damn man fought her at every turn on that score. It was like he enjoyed wallowing in his misery.

And secondly, Nick was just plain hauntingly gor-geous. That probably shouldn't matter, but it certainly did. His hair, a mixed shade of golden blond with silver streaks, had grown slightly too long, like hers, and brushed his collar. He had a slender build, and at six foot two he towered over her five foot four inch frame.

Nick usually wore boring but expensive gray or navy clothes, even to work out in. But even in dull-colored clothes, the spectacular blue of his eyes always fascinated her. Just as it was doing now, while he shot her a forbidden look that blazed with anger at her interruption.

It couldn't be helped. Irritating as he may be, it was her job to stick with him and make sure he took care of himself. She was nothing if not loyal and trustworthy. But heaven help her, this was a man who stirred her senses like no man had ever done before.

"I'll go indoors if *you* will," she told him when she got close enough to be heard. "The storm is almost here. It's too dangerous to be outside."

The waves had grown tall all of a sudden, she noted. Ever since she'd come to the island, Annie had loved the quiet easy way the surf here rolled in, baby-soft against the beach. The waves were usually like a child, tenderly caressing its mother's hair with long smooth strokes.

But today the adult waves crashed and thundered against the shallow depths of their sheltered cove. Angry white caps rose up to impossible heights and smacked down with fury against the bottom. The beautiful blues and greens she'd grown accustomed to seeing when she looked out at the ocean had disappeared—replaced by tan-colored water that boiled and stirred, and resembled her grandmother's chicken gravy.

Despite the heat and humidity, Annie shivered.

"The dolphins will be all right, won't they?" she asked, holding out her hand to him.

"I'm concerned about Sultana," Nick said roughly. "She is expected to give birth within days and it will be our first live birth at the center. But every precaution that could be taken seems to have been completed." He didn't accept her hand, but clasped his own hands behind his back instead.

The storm was in his eyes today, and it made him seem so much more human. And at the moment, much more annoying.

Nick desperately wanted a few more minutes by himself. It was bad enough that the storm had ruined his plans for the day—this day of all days. The thought of being helpless to assist the research team during the storm also made him remember too clearly another time when he had not been able to help.

Absently rubbing his temple, he felt the familiar ache of memories.

But the worst thing about this storm was knowing he had to spend the rest of the day…and night…alone with Annie. Damn the storm. And damn her.

She got under his skin and he didn't like it one bit. He was a one-woman man and his woman had been violently taken from him. Other women, no matter how inviting, were distractions he just didn't need.

He needed to remain frozen and apart. Distance let him maintain his emotional balance. Cold hearts didn't feel guilt. Being numb meant keeping the pain at bay.

Nick had spent two long years keeping his distance

from life, and damned if Annie didn't bring that tempting heat right onto the island with her. Heat and wanting.

Hell, he just hated these emotions. But he knew his mother would have a fit if he fired Annie. She thought Annie was good for him. Another few weeks of Annie's perky helpfulness, however, and he might just explode.

His only hope tonight was if he could talk Annie into remaining in her room at the back of the house while he spent the long hours of the storm by himself in his office. He was already restless but it had nothing to do with the coming storm.

The anniversary of Christina's death made him feel unsettled and uneasy. He wanted to be left alone so he could bring back the sharp pain of missing her.

That pain brought her memory into clear focus and reminded him of all his vows and promises. All the promises he had never been able to keep while his wife was alive. He needed those memories to stay focused now.

"But she'll be okay, won't she? Sultana is healthy, you said." Annie withdrew her hand but took a step closer.

Her voice brought him back to the moment with a thud. Nodding, he backed up a step to keep from touching the vibrant personal trainer.

Lately, every time Annie touched him, he burned—and he was surprised by his growing attraction to her. He didn't want any part of the lustful urges.

Nick had tried desperately to keep his distance from Annie over the past few weeks, and had worked hard to manage his exercises by his own strength. But she *was* a personal trainer, and had kept her watchful eyes and sensual hands on his body as he exercised in his home gym.

He groaned silently at the very thought. His unruly desire for her was getting so bad, he had actually considered risking his mother's wrath by hiring someone else in her place.

Though Annie was strictly his employee, on his mother's frequent visits, the two women had become friends. Coconspirators against him, he supposed.

It was bad enough that his father was furious with him for quitting the business to come live on the island and devote himself to Christina's project. Nick didn't want to risk losing his mother's support, too.

Family was all important. But as much as he loved his mother, she was a meddler.

Since his wife's death two years ago, his mind was often distracted. That was only one of the several reasons he'd left his home in Alsaca and given up everything he'd ever worked to achieve. He'd come to honor Christina's memory and wishes in the very place where she had died.

But his mother was unduly worried about his isolation and absentmindedness. And he knew she thought Annie could bring him back to the world of the living.

In his opinion, Annie was *entirely* too alive.

"Please come with me, Nick," Annie said as she looked up at him with those spectacular emerald eyes, flashing in both vivid color and obvious heat.

He had never seen a woman with such vibrance and fire. It fascinated him how different from Christina she was. Of how different Annie was from any woman in his experience.

But he couldn't let her touch him. Not while he was

so vulnerable today. He had to find a way to push her away, make her leave him alone.

"All right. You go ahead. I'll be right behind you," he said in his most demanding voice.

She screwed up her wide, full mouth in a frown for a second. But then she swung around and took a couple of steps toward the house before turning back to make sure he was following.

He started out, but soon realized that he'd made a huge mistake. He should've taken the lead. That way he wouldn't be stuck walking behind her and admiring the way she looked as she swung her hips in those sexy, too-short white shorts.

Even in the dull light of the prestorm sky, Annie was radiant and energetic enough to make him forget his vows of celibacy since his wife's death. She made him think instead of how he would dearly love to run his fingers through that mass of fiery red curls. Or to place his lips against the adorable rusty freckles that spattered across her nose like paint spills.

Her energy snapped about her as if she were static electricity during a thunderstorm. He found himself nearly drooling at the thought of capturing her to him and tasting all that vividness.

Instead, he fisted his hands and stuck them in his pockets. Concentrating on what hurricane preparations might be left to attend to and on how ferocious the storm might actually become, he vowed to keep his growing lust a secret.

He'd always thought that sex was a sacred trust. One best shared only once in a lifetime and mostly for procreation. Fidelity and honor meant more than mere bodily urges. And he would not betray Christina's memory by jumping the first woman that had turned him on since her death.

Annie stirred the stockpot on the range as she heard the first tinkling sounds of rain against the shuttered windows. Before he left for the mainland, the chef had given her instructions for keeping herself and Nick fed during the storm and its aftermath.

The freezer was stocked with things that could be defrosted and heated up on the outdoor barbeque grill after the storm. She was making a big pot of her mother's Irish stew that could be reheated on a small propane gas stove during the storm if the island's electricity went out.

Annie could hear Nick in the other parts of house as he rummaged around, locating kerosene lamps, flashlights and candles. She didn't worry about his physical ability to move through the house anymore. Not like she had when she'd first come and he'd been so unsteady on his injured knee.

It had taken all her knowledge of anatomic kinesiology and experience with physical conditioning in people with limited mobility to help him reestablish the strength in his legs. And then, of course, there had been the whole problem of motivation. Every time she'd pushed him a little further than the time before, he'd blazed with anger and backed away from her, almost as if her touch had somehow burned him.

Lately, the tension in the air between them was thick enough to make her more nervous than she liked to admit.

"Would you care to join me in a cup of tea?"

The sound of his voice startled her and she dropped the spoon into the stew pot. "Darn. You surprised me. Don't sneak up on me like that."

He reached for a pair of tongs from the round carousel that held kitchen utensils. "Sorry." Dipping the tongs in the stew, he retrieved the spoon, wiped it off with a towel and handed it back to her with a polite bow. "Here you are, *mademoiselle*. No harm done."

"Pretty slick, Nick, and how very European of you. I didn't realize you were so familiar with a kitchen. I just imagined you'd always had a chef and would barely be able to find the kitchen, let alone know where things were kept in one."

"Don't tell anyone," he said with a frown. "I've been sneaking into the kitchen for most of my life. Ever since I found out that's where the sweets are kept."

Annie giggled, put the lid back on the pot and turned the heat down under it. "If you're serious about making tea, I'd love some."

"Certainly," he said with a formal air. He began opening jars and putting fresh water into the tea kettle.

She stood aside to watch him work and waited, she supposed, for him to drop something or in some other way need her help. Which she knew would not make him happy.

Sure enough, her hovering angered him. "Sit down. This will take a few minutes." The darn man intimidated her, but she couldn't let him know that.

She did as he asked and sat at the narrow kitchen table, but the nervous energy spilled off her like rapids over a waterfall. "I didn't mean to make you uncomfortable. I'm just not used to sitting while someone else works. I really appreciate you letting me stay here with you through the storm. I never would've been able to stand being in the U.S. not knowing if you were okay."

Her words gushed out. "I mean, I've never been through a hurricane before. Is it going to be terrifying? I think we're all set, don't you? Should I be doing something?"

"Calm down." He turned away from the counter. "You're becoming hysterical. Everything will be fine, trust me," he said with a rare smile.

There it was again. Lately whenever he smiled, an odd feeling that a big change was coming flew through her mind and heart. She'd been having these mystical sensory imaginings for days—no maybe it was weeks now.

It was something her mother would no doubt call Irish intuition. Fate appeared to be poised for stepping in and stirring its own pot of mischief.

But Annie was sure whatever it was couldn't be connected to the impending storm. The hurricane had been planned for and watched over for days. No, this would be some major change for her and Nick personally, she felt it in her bones.

Hw was much healthier now than when she'd first arrived on the island and better able to take care of himself. Maybe he was considering letting her go. That wouldn't be too much of a shock, even though it would make her sad to have to leave him. But she'd known all along that this was not a permanent assignment.

"Do you always talk so fast when you're nervous?"

"Yes. I guess I do." She watched as he moved smoothly around the stainless steel kitchen, putting together tea and water and then setting china cups on the table.

The man was going to use real china for their casual tea. Wouldn't Ma think that was something?

He set the silver teapot down to steep on a little cart next to the table, and then he pulled out a chair and sat down beside her. "There's no need to be worried about the storm, Annie. I've been through several hurricanes. Proper preparation is the key. Most storms are not direct hits and end up just being long, boring ordeals."

She wasn't nervous about the storm. If she was worried about anything, it was the fantasies she'd been having lately about the man who was her boss and the possibility that soon she might never be able to see him again.

Sitting next to him now was making her thighs tingle. And wasn't that an odd thing?

"Would you like biscuits with your tea?" he asked.

She shook her head and tried a half smile. He was close enough that she was catching his scent. The smell of salt spray, a whiff of some expensive aftershave and the musk of a light sheen of sweat lingered in the air and made her feel warm and itchy. There was something wild in that combination that she didn't quite recognize, but today it was definitely doing strange things to her body.

"You know why I didn't want you to stay here on the island during the storm?" he asked as he poured the tea.

"You weren't worried about my safety."

"No. I'd planned to ask you and the rest of the staff to leave me and go down to the village today so I could be alone in the house," he said. "The storm put a crimp in my plans."

"You wanted to be alone today?" She knew this was

a special day for him. But if it had been her, trying to get through the anniversary of the death of a loved one, she would've wanted all her family and friends around for support.

He tilted his chin with a sharp nod. "It's just a little ritual of honor that I began last year that helps me bid Christina goodbye again. A commemoration I suppose you'd call it."

"Will that be all ruined now?"

Nick studied her for a moment. "Not if I can help it. Since you have insisted on staying on the island, I want you to spend the balance of the night in your suite alone. You should be able to find things to occupy your time there while I'm in my office."

He was such an annoying prickly loner of a man. "I guess that would be okay," she said through gritted teeth. "As long as you promise to call me if you need anything."

On the other hand, who could complain about being alone in that fabulous suite with her CD player and the luxury of being able to read her books without being interrupted? It had been a dream of hers since she'd been a little girl.

Not that she hadn't loved growing up in a houseful of kids, but family sometimes became so overwhelming.

"Just try to sleep through the storm, Annie. It's the easiest way. The whole affair is usually so dull."

She would never mention it to him, but nothing could ever be dull while he was around. He had created a gray world for himself here, but her world had been full of nothing but exciting living color ever since the day they'd first met.

Two

After dinner, Annie cleared the dishes, put the pans into the sink and ran water over them. "Would you like coffee with your dessert?"

"Yes, thanks," Nick answered as he stood and backed away from the kitchen table. "Is there something I can do to help?" He needed to get this damn meal over with so he could be alone.

She laughed and the sound lingered in the air, stirring his blood as if she were a real-life wizard with a magic wand. "You volunteering to do the dishes, Nick? I can just see that now. It would be almost as odd as seeing you eating dinner in the kitchen with me has been."

"Well, perhaps I might be slightly too fumble-fingered to actually wash. But I feel competent enough to dry the dishes if you wish."

He'd actually liked eating in the kitchen at the same

table with her. It had been strangely cozy and warm. And as much as he wanted to be alone, prolonging the intimacy for just a little longer might not be so terrible.

Besides, drying dishes would give him something to do with his hands as he tried to get his needs under control.

Using the back of her suds covered hand, Annie flipped the hair back off her shoulder. "I'm going to let them soak. Until you…retire for the duration of the storm. Just let me set the coffeepot up, then I'll get the lime custard pie out of the refrigerator and flame the meringue."

"You know how to do that?"

She tsked at him. "I've been taking cooking lessons from your French chef. I even wrote down the instructions."

"I can't imagine that you'd want lessons in cooking," he said unwarily as he finished the coffee. "Didn't you tell me that you came from a big Irish family? I thought…"

"What?" she interrupted as she stood still and glared at him. "That poor kids from the other side of the tracks had better learn to feed themselves? Or maybe that all Irishmen ate nothing but boiled potatoes and wouldn't be interested in French cooking."

"No, not at all. I didn't mean…" Whatever he'd said was the wrong thing and he didn't know how to make it right.

Annie shook her head and then smiled. "Never mind. I overreacted. Sorry. Sit down and I'll start the show."

She lit the small propane torch, ran the flame over the white fluffy top of the pie and the smell of burnt sugar suddenly filled the air. "Oh, by all the saints, how I love the way that smells," she moaned.

And oh how he loved the way she had closed her eyes and groaned in pleasure. It was a sensual, earthy sound that put stinging darts of desire right down his spine.

But he desperately needed to stop listening and look-ing…stop everything when it came to her. This was all wrong. He simply could not sit here lusting after her. For him to even promote their burgeoning friendship would be dishonorable.

His feelings toward her ran too strong. If there was one thing he had learned in his life, it was that friend-ships didn't last. And when they were ripped away, a huge part of your soul went with them.

No, friendship and love were illusions. He had never in his life been in love and didn't even have the foggi-est idea what that emotion would be like. His one and only friendship had been with Christina and that had ob-viously worked out in the worst possible way.

So Nick was determined to keep his distance from Annie. He had even come to the conclusion that after the hurricane, he would be forced to let her go. Before it was too late.

When the dessert was perfectly browned, Annie poured the coffee and sat down at the table with him. Her eyes blazed as she lifted the fork and drew hot sugar and cold custard into her mouth.

"This is so decadent. My mother would call this combination of tastes a sin."

Only one of the many ways of putting yourself in hell, Nick thought. He had to get her talking. Sitting close and watching her lick the sugar off her lips was slowly but very surely sending him straight to the devil.

"Tell me about your mother," he said as he pushed his half-eaten dessert aside. "Tell me about your whole family."

She looked up at him with wide eyes. "Really? There's a gazillion of them. It might take some time."

"A gazillion?" he asked with a chuckle. "How many is that exactly?"

"Well, I've told you that I have three brothers and three sisters...all older. My mother is one of ten children, and my father is the youngest of thirteen. And I have nine nieces and nephews and sixty cousins—so far."

"I guess that does qualify as a gazillion. I was an only child. I have a couple of cousins that live in the U.S., but I can't really imagine having as much family as you. Do you all live near each other in Boston?"

"Mostly," she said as she pushed her empty plate aside and took a sip of coffee. "Two of my cousins joined the army and went off for a while. But when their hitches were up, they came right back home to settle down.

"I do have one daring uncle who took his family back to the homeland to live," she continued. "Claimed he could only breathe the air if he was in Ireland."

Nick caught the sour facial expression. "Interesting. Ever give much thought to moving to Ireland yourself?"

"Me? No. It would be too much like home—everyone knows everyone else's business and has to put their two cents worth into it."

"Your family are gossips?"

"It's more like they all just read each other's minds…and then don't like what they see and insist on correcting the other person's shortcomings. My mother is the worst of the lot." She said the last with a twinkle in her eyes.

"My mother tends to be a busybody, too."

"*Your* mother is a saint! You have no idea what a professional 'stick-her-nose-in' can be like."

He laughed, maybe harder than he had in years. Maybe ever. Annie was a true gem. A tempting emerald set in a ruby cluster, and he was beginning to covet her more than he should—much more than he could stand at the moment.

"Tell me about what it was like to grow up with so many brothers and sisters," he said quickly when his thoughts strayed off the topic again.

She shrugged and sighed. "There's good things and bad about it."

"Tell me something good."

"You are never lonely."

"Well, that sounds nice. Now tell me something bad."

"You are never lonely," she said with a wicked grin.

Nick smiled but Annie could see shadows behind his eyes. She knew he was lonely. He'd locked himself up here on his island and had spent so many hours alone since his wife had died that it was a small wonder he still knew how to speak to other human beings at all.

He did speak to her, though. He spoke straight to her heart—with words or without. She could feel his pain in her chest right now.

But she knew she wouldn't be the one to break the

spell on him. What he needed was some sophisticated blond princess, not a scraggly redheaded Irish kid from the poor side of town.

"Why do you spend all your time alone, Nick?" she asked brazenly, trying to break his bad mood. "You're like a prince who's been put under a spell. It seems you should have friends…and girlfriends. I can't understand why you don't."

"My friend…the one woman who was my only girlfriend and my wife…died," he said softly. "It would dishonor her memory if I…" He stopped and looked guilt-stricken.

"You don't have to tell me, Nick. I really don't need to understand. It's your life." She watched the deep blue in his eyes turn stormy. "But I'm a good listener in case you need one."

He hung his head and silently stared down into his coffee cup.

"My grandmother is a very great lady," Annie hurriedly told him with a small laugh. "And really old. She always says that it's good to talk about people who have gone on to heaven before us. Talking about them keeps their memories fresh and alive. Telling stories about lost loved ones is a way to see them clearly in your mind and to bring them closer to your heart again."

Nick gave her a small shake of his head but didn't look up or make a sound.

"Of course, Gran doesn't just tell stories about family and friends," Annie added. "Once she starts the stories, she goes on to tell the ones she learned in her childhood in Ireland. Those are wonderful stories about mysticism and magic—elves and sorcerers. I could…"

"I met a woman with magic," Nick interrupted. "It was in New Orleans six months ago right before I hired you."

Annie silently gave a sigh of relief. He was actually talking again. Thank heaven.

"She was an old gypsy and she gave me a book," he added with a scowl.

"A book?"

Nick nodded once and his eyes became glazed. "It was the oddest thing. She gave me this obviously expensive and antique book and said it was my destiny. But then she disappeared before she told me why."

"What kind of a book?"

"The cover says it's the original Grimm's stories."

"The fairy tales?"

"I suppose so."

"But you haven't opened it?"

"No. I didn't think that fairy tales were my kind of reading material." He'd said that softly, almost wistfully, and it made Annie more than a little curious.

Interesting—and completely confusing. "So how do you know this old gypsy woman had magic?"

"I…I'm not sure. I just felt it. I think the book is magic, too."

"But you haven't read it yet?"

"You may read it if you want. I'll let you see it sometime."

He was somehow nervous about the magic, she thought with a sudden insight. But considering her background, *she* wasn't afraid of gypsies or magic. Just curious.

Nick had actually told her about something important to him, though. Annie thought that might be some kind of breakthrough, so she tried a friendly push to keep him talking.

"I'd rather hear your story than read one," she told him. "Tell me about Christina. Talk about how you two met." She'd put her hand on his forearm to let him feel how much she cared, but the electric shock she felt when she'd touched his skin made her draw the hand back in a hurry.

Annie got up and began to casually clear their dessert dishes with feigned indifference. She knew she was probably being pushy with a man who was her boss, and she didn't want this to seem like an interrogation. But he needed to talk.

And she needed to get over whatever these odd feelings were toward him. Even though he was sometimes infuriating, he was a nice man and obviously hurting. And she just wanted to help—not jump him.

"Um…well, Christina's father and my father were old friends—more business partners than friends, I guess you would say. My father does not cultivate friends that serve no purpose." He'd said that with a rather strangled sound in his voice, but Annie had her back to him and couldn't see his expression.

She let him talk while she busied herself at the sink.

"Anyway, Christina and I knew each other all of our lives," he said quietly. "When I was old enough to leave Europe for the United States to attend university preparatory school, Father informed me that our families would be well served if the two of us were joined."

He took a deep breath, and it was all Annie could do not to turn around to see his face. "I understood his point completely and recognized my obligation," he began again. "And spoke to Christina about our future so that we would have an understanding before I left Alsaca."

That did it. Annie spun around. "You became engaged as teenagers? Just like that?"

He looked up at her with slight confusion in his eyes. "Yes, of course. I know that isn't the way it's done in the United States, but in Europe it's quite common for two prominent families to join like that."

"But what about love?"

"Christina and I had a close relationship. We had always been friends. It was just natural."

Natural, maybe, Annie thought. But definitely not romantic. She sighed softly. What about the magic? But she managed to kept her mouth shut.

Nick got up and moved to the sink to stand beside her. He picked up a towel. "If you've changed your mind about washing the dishes now, may I help?"

Annie looked down at the sink and realized she'd been washing and stacking the dishes while she listened to him talk. "I guess so. If you really want to."

"Yes. The time goes by faster if you stay busy."

How right he was. Annie had learned that lesson early in a home where too much time on your hands only brought more teasing from older siblings.

"So how long were you two married?" she asked as she handed him a dish.

"We celebrated our fourth wedding anniversary right before…"

Oops. "Four years?" she broke in hurriedly. "Boy, that's so short a time. But you didn't have any kids?"

"No." The answer came slowly, almost as if it pained him just to admit it.

Annie figured she'd managed to make one more mistake with her big, fat mouth. But never let it be said that she knew when to just shut up.

"I'll bet you two were so busy with your lives and being newlyweds that you didn't want children to intrude on your happiness. Kids can be a real pain."

"On the contrary, Christina…we…wanted very badly to have a child. The doctors told us it would be impossible for either one of us to have a natural child of our own."

He finished drying a plate and carefully put it aside. "And before you ask, Annie" he added wryly. "I suggested that we adopt. But Christina could never…I think the American saying is 'come to grips with the idea.'"

"I'm sorry. That must've been difficult."

"Christina… Well, she was devastated. But it spurred her into planning for the creation of this marine mammal research center. It was a project that had been very dear to her for many years."

"Your family has owned this island for a long time?"

"Generations. But my grandfather deeded the village over to the citizens about fifty years ago. Most of the islander families have worked for my family through the years and Grandfather wanted to repay them for their loyalty."

It must be nice to be rich enough to give away a whole town. Annie's family couldn't afford to give away so much as a seashell.

"You finished the research facility when your wife drowned, didn't you? I mean, it might've been her idea but you were the one that did the work to get it opened."

"I wanted—" He stopped drying dishes and put the towel down. "I wanted to find a way to give her what she had desired. I could not give her the child of her dreams, but I could see to it that her dream of doing this research went on in her honor."

His hurt and guilt about not being able to have a child shone quite clearly in his eyes. Poor guy.

"And you were physically injured yourself at the time. You must've loved her very much." Annie could feel a single tear escaping from her eye, and tried to keep any more from embarrassing her by sniffing and lowering her chin.

Instead of an answer, Nick turned to Annie and lifted her chin so she was forced to look up into his eyes. He tenderly wiped away the lone tear, then pushed a wayward curl back behind her ear.

"I think perhaps it would be best if I retire to my office now. Thank you for the lovely meal. I don't believe the hurricane should cause you too many problems."

"Oh, I'll be just fine," she said quickly. His touch had driven a jolt straight to her toes and she needed to step back from him and think about what had happened.

"Yes, I'm sure I will be fine, as well." He dropped his hand to his side and moved quickly toward the kitchen door. "Good night, Annie."

"Don't forget to let me know if you need anything," she called after him.

But he was gone. And she was already beginning to feel cold in his absence—as if stabbing fingers of lonely icicles were reaching right down into her gut and turning her inside out.

Three

Nick picked up the decanter and poured himself a snifter of brandy. His office, with its rich masculine colors, black slate tiles and warm suede sofa and chairs, normally gave him solace. But not tonight.

His thoughts kept turning to Annie—to how she would handle the hurricane alone back in her rooms. And damned if he also couldn't help but wonder what she might be wearing as she retired for the night.

Did she wear one of those frilly, see-through contraptions that some women liked to wear to bed? If so, he knew it would be silky soft but full of wild, exotic tones, just like Annie herself. Her nightwear would never be simple white or black, he was positive.

For Annie, the hue would have to be a deep, forest green to match her eyes—or perhaps a vibrant turquoise like the waters here in the Caribbean. He could even imagine her in a blast of lipstick-red or a cool Mediterranean-coral that would complement her coloring.

Shaking his head, he put the glass to his lips and let the warm, liquid fire ease down his throat. He shouldn't be doing this, having indecent thoughts about a woman who was his employee. It wasn't particularly honorable nor faithful to the memory of his wife.

But what if Annie wore a T-shirt to bed? Or perhaps she wore nothing at all.

The stab of heat that image brought cut him clear down to his gut. He slouched on the office's wide, comfortable sofa and glanced over to the framed photograph of Christina that sat on the end table beside him.

His wife's cool, blond image stared back. He'd always loved the way Christina's sophisticated hairstyles had matched her polished method of dressing. She'd seemed to him to be the perfect fragile, silver angel. But he'd never felt the sharp pang of desire for Christina that the mere thought of Annie's clothes could bring to him.

Nor had he ever felt any emotion that might qualify as love for her. No matter how badly he'd wanted to feel it at the time.

He closed his eyes and waited for the familiar melancholy to settle over him. Thirty years old, and he had only had sex with one woman in his entire lifetime. Some men would think that was an old-fashioned ideal, but he had never wanted there to be anyone else but his wife. And now that he knew he was incapable of having children, it was the only honorable thing to do.

It irritated him that tonight, when he should be remembering ethereal Christina's flawless face and the consuming way she had loved the sea, all he could picture in his mind was earthy Annie and the sound of her laughter as it wafted through the air and settled low in his body.

Annie was pure temptation, tempting him to leave behind his safe gray world. Her eyes were hypnotic, her voice the siren sound of sensual desire.

Banishing all thoughts of her, Nick stood and poured himself another brandy. Then he turned and lifted his glass toward his wife's photograph.

"Here's to you, darling," he toasted. "I've kept all my promises. Your marine mammal center is fully functional and I will make sure only the best research is ever done there."

He took a sip and let the guilt run down his throat. "And I'm sorry I couldn't be everything you needed while you were alive. I couldn't give you the child you so desired and I pushed you to be what I expected you to be."

He'd left out a big part of Christina's story when he'd told it to Annie. Deliberately, he'd neglected to tell her about the pain, the anger and the cold doubts about Christina's death.

Waiting for the icy ache of dislocation that usually came over him when he thought about his lost wife's missed opportunities, he noticed instead that he just felt numb. Unlike last year's ritual of goodbye, this year the pain of the loss had softened around the edges. It had become indistinct and blurry.

He needed that sharp pain to return. To remind him of the emptiness—and of his promises.

Downing the second glass of brandy, Nick poured himself another. It was almost the time for his agreed-upon call to the research center to check on their progress with the storm.

The idea that the dolphins might be helpless if they happened to escape the lagoon where they were raised gave him cold chills. But once again there was nothing he could do to keep the sea from wreaking whatever havoc it chose to inflict. At this point, he was much more helpless in the ocean than the dolphins.

As he headed for his desk phone, Nick caught sight of the gypsy's book. He reached out to touch it, but withdrew his hand when the book felt warm to his touch. Not tonight.

Nick wasn't quite ready to face children's fairy tales tonight. Now that he knew he would never be a father, any reminder of what he would be missing seemed too cruel.

The gypsy said the book would bring him to his heart's desire. Not likely. Rather, tales of love and happily ever after would only bring him more pain.

Turning away from the book, he decided that after the call was made, he and the decanter of Napoleon were going to spend some quality time on the sofa, riding out the storm. And trying to control any wayward thoughts of Annie.

She was just another reminder of all the things he could never have.

"Oh, no you don't," Passionata Chagari warned as she stared down into her crystal ball.

This brash young Scoville was determined to ignore the magic. But the old gypsy woman would not let him get away with that.

She was not supposed to stir into the future, but to Hades with regulations. Thinking of ways to move him on toward his destiny, Passionata concentrated on the ultimate goal.

The hurricane… Yes, perhaps their safe refuge had a weak spot. Something that would bring Nicholas closer to the truth, yet would not damage his self-image for the time being.

The young man had a lot to learn and a lot to unlearn. And this old gypsy using her father's magic was just the person who could teach him the lessons.

The lights flickered one more time and Annie set the book down beside her on the bed and stared at the bed-side lamp. Maybe if she kept a careful watch on it for a few minutes, the electricity would hold still long enough for her to finish one more chapter.

She'd been having some difficulty concentrating on the wonderful new romance novel that her sister Brenna had sent in a care package that had arrived just yesterday. Bless Brenna, Annie thought. Chocolate bars, fingernail polish, a bar of vanilla-scented soap and a new novel by her favorite author. What more could a person want?

Annie glanced at her newly polished toenails and smiled. The island village did have a small grocery store that carried the basics. But they certainly didn't carry blue nail polish.

The sounds of the storm caught her attention as it intensified outside the walls of her room. The winds roared and tree branches whipped against the roof and windows. She felt safe and secure here in her suite, though.

This whole single-story wing of the house was brand-new, built within the past five years. Everything was so fresh and clean with its seashell motif and the beige and white paint, bedspread and drapes. Much more sophisticated than her room back home.

Her gaze landed back on the open book beside her. It was a terrific romance. But she couldn't read more than a paragraph or two without thinking about Nick.

For weeks now, she'd been having dreamy fantasies about her boss. She'd tried to squelch them. Fantasizing about her boss was a complication that felt way beyond her abilities.

But every time she closed her eyes, his silky blond hair with its silver tips and his wide sensual mouth kept creeping into her mind, making her fingers burn to touch them. Along with some other parts of him that she wouldn't want to admit, even to herself.

And every time recently that the two of them had been close enough to touch in real life, she'd felt giddy and nervous and not at all like her normal self. She'd even noticed that she'd been giggling and sweating whenever he came close. For heaven's sake.

She'd given it a lot of thought. Regardless of how irritating Nick could be at times, this just had to be a real old-fashioned crush. She had certainly seen her older sisters go through similar things enough times.

As teens in an all girls' school, her sisters had never been interested in anything else but boys. They'd begged to be let out on dates. Their strict parents had tried to keep the gates locked and the temptations to a minimum, but her sisters had found sneaky ways around the rules.

During her own teen years, Annie had gossiped on the phone with girlfriends and dreamed about a Prince Charming coming to sweep her off her feet. But she'd been too focused on her athletic teams, her studies and her books to work all that hard on finding boyfriends. In high school, getting an athletic scholarship to college had been her biggest goal.

She had dated a few times in college, but she'd been so busy thinking up a way out of the house and out of Boston that it hadn't left much time to worry about finding the perfect man. After college, her dreams had slowly turned to a desperation for travel, seeing the world and all the wonderful and far-off places she'd been reading about all her life.

"And boy did I get more than I'd ever thought possible," she said aloud to her empty designer room.

Nick's Caribbean island was like something out of one of her favorite novels. She was doing what she'd always dreamed of doing. So the idea of being caught up in her first real crush at the age of twenty-four was a bit much.

Silly, she mused. She'd better dig down deep and find some of that practical good sense, just like her mother had always cautioned. Nick was about as attainable as one of her fairy-tale princes.

Throughout the evening, the storm battered the roof and the sides of the house with pelting rains and gale force winds. Nick awakened several times to the sounds of something heavy hitting the house.

At midnight he prowled through the darkened main house, worrying about the dolphins in their protected lagoon. The storm had turned course slightly and they were catching more of the hurricane than anyone had predicted.

The electricity had gone out about an hour ago and he had not been able to reach any of the research team since then. Using a flashlight, he entered the kitchen and immediately his thoughts turned from dolphins to Annie. Dammit. Not again. He had to stop this.

Just then, a tremendous noise echoed through the house, loud enough to be heard above the storm.

Nick turned and made his way in the dark to Annie's quarters as fast as he could. He threw open the hallway door and barged right into her rooms, yelling at the top of his lungs.

"Annie! Where are you?" He flipped the beam of the flashlight around but found only an empty bed.

The sounds of the storm had grown louder in here and he could feel the air stirring. He turned toward the source of the wind and bolted to the open bathroom door, reaching it with little trouble in the dark.

But when he stepped inside the threshold, he found chaos. A huge palm tree lay half-inside the bathroom while the other half was still caught by the corner of the roof. But there were fronds and broken glass and now rainwater building higher on the tile floor.

And Annie stood on the counter in the middle of it all, trying to shove bath towels into the hole in the roof.

He swore once then moved toward her through the debris. "Are you all right? Just leave the damned thing alone and come away from there."

"I don't have my shoes. I think I already cut my foot on the glass," she hollered above the roar of the rains.

"Then put your arms around my neck. I'll carry you."

"You can't carry me! I'm too heavy," she protested.

He waded closer to the counter. "My personal trainer would disagree with you on that one. She says I'm a lot stronger than I look." He'd said it with a forced smile as he reached to tug her down into his waiting arms, but he was too concerned about her safety to be very gentle.

Annie rolled against his chest and hooked an arm around his neck. Holding onto the flashlight with one hand, he pressed her close. She was as light as a baby in his protective embrace—and soaking wet from standing in the rain that was coming in through the roof.

Slick and cool against his naked, warm chest, Annie's body slipped lower against his abdomen. He groaned silently and begged for strength. The friction of her skin rubbing against his skin was causing him to lose his mind.

Carrying her, Nick quickly stepped into the bedroom and slammed the bathroom door behind him. He gently let her slide the rest of the way down his body to the bed.

"The bathroom is a mess, and I'm worried about the integrity of the roof on this whole section of the house," he told her as he stepped back and let the flashlight illuminate the room. "Let's get you some dry clothes and then you and I will have to spend the rest of the hurricane in my office. It's in a part of the house that's been through several previous hurricanes and should be safe enough."

"Yessir, master," she quipped as she prepared to get off the bed.

"Cute. But stay put." Nick put a hand on her shoulder and gently pushed her back down. "Just tell me where to look for your things. You shouldn't stand until we have a chance to attend to your cut foot."

Frustrated, Annie scowled up at him. "I can get around by myself. I've always excelled at one-footed races."

"Stay there," he demanded once again and moved to her closet. "We have to hurry. Tell me what you need."

Annie directed him to the drawer with her shorts and T-shirts. Then she watched as he and the light disappeared into the huge walk-in closet. She would've liked to have dry underwear too, but simply could not imagine having him sift through her bras and panties.

Nick was back in an instant. "You carry your clothes and the light," he ordered as he shoved shirt, shorts and flashlight into her hands. "I'll carry you."

Once more, he lifted her easily. She closed her eyes for a second, much too aware of where his body was touching hers. But the flashlight was in her possession, so she opened her eyes and tried to keep the beam steady, showing him the way through the darkened house.

His arm was tight around her back, while her side was pressed against his firm naked chest. She wasn't accustomed to seeing him without a shirt. He'd always worn T-shirts to work out.

The muscles that she'd help create, bulged and bunched as he moved them past darkened obstacles. She tightened her grip around his neck and clung to him as she felt herself slipping down his body. Both of them were sweating and slick in the heat and humidity.

He dragged her up closer and she caught a whiff of something that smelled like good old-fashioned soap, coming from his sweat-glistened skin. The familiar scent seemed unbelievably masculine all of a sudden.

An electric tingle rushed across her skin and she could barely breathe. Having him carry her in his arms had turned into one of the most erotic experiences of her entire lifetime.

A few moments later, Nick entered a guest bathroom that she'd never been in before. "I'm going to let you down now. Do you think you can change clothes on one foot while I go locate the first aid kit?"

He bent to help her keep steady on her one good leg. But as she slid down his body, she felt the unmistakable thrust of aroused male against her back. She twisted and grabbed for his shoulders, shaken by her own desire as much as by his.

"Uh…hold on to the counter," Nick said roughly. "Everything will be fine as soon as you change and I doctor your wound.

"Keep the light with you," he urged with a rush as he stepped away and thrust a dry towel at her. "I can find my way in the dark to get another flashlight."

"But, Nick…"

Whatever she would've said to make him take the light with him was lost. He disappeared into the darkened hallway and left her all alone to wonder what had caused both of them to totally lose their senses.

"Let me look at your foot, Annie." Nick was standing before her as she sat on the edge of the bathroom counter.

His body took up all the air and space in what she'd thought before was a huge room. He'd brought the first aid kit and a kerosene lantern back with him. Being able to see his expression and his steel-blue eyes was not helping her feel any less nervous.

She lifted her foot toward him before remembering her new toenail polish. It was too late now.

"I tried to wash the cut while I was waiting for you to come back," she said with a shaky voice.

He turned her foot in his warm hands and stared down at her toes. "What color is that? Blue?" It felt so strange, having him touching her bare foot that way.

She'd hoped that he would never have to see her little girly choice of polish. How embarrassing. She should be wearing her athletic shoes, like she nearly always did.

"My sister sent it to me. I was just messing around tonight while I waited out the storm. It's not my usual color. I—"

"I like it on you," he interrupted with a raspy chuckle. "It's fresh and full of energy. Just like you."

"Oh." Annie was totally overwhelmed by the heat she'd seen in his eyes.

Nick still had hold of her foot. Suddenly she realized what was happening. She was aroused by having him touch her bare skin. And if she didn't miss her guess, Nick was aroused as well. Jeez. Now what?

"The cut doesn't look too deep," he told her as he studied it. "Do you think you washed all the glass out?"

"I'm pretty sure."

He raised his eyes to question her and she was immediately struck dumb by his nearness. His face was mere inches from her own. If she just leaned forward slightly, she could kiss those full lips. She could reach out and pull him in for the pleasure of it.

Her imagination began to run away with her and ripples of some unnamed sensation ran down her spine as he began to bandage her feet. It was too intense and she closed her eyes so he wouldn't guess what she was thinking.

Nick had to bite the inside of his cheek in order to get through bandaging Annie's wound. It was all he could do not to ravish her right there in the bathroom.

It had been easy to see that she wanted him. If not because of the sexy bedroom way she'd been staring at his lips, then because of the way her nipples had peaked against the thin material of her T-shirt as he tended to her wound.

Obviously, she wasn't wearing a bra. But then, he remembered that she'd been in her silky shorty pajamas when the roof had caved in. Of course she wouldn't wear a bra to bed. And he hadn't retrieved any underwear for her on their way out of her suite.

Knowing that was driving him crazy. He didn't want to stare at her chest. It had been tough enough before when she'd felt his arousal against her back. Good Lord. Male anatomy was such a pain sometimes.

It was a huge relief to finally have her bandaged and safe and sound on the sofa in his office. Now he had to find something to do to keep them both occupied through the rest of this storm.

He absolutely refused to give in to his body's demands. He was a much better man than that.

"Do you want to try to get some sleep? That sofa is fairly comfortable," he asked with too much force.

"Are you kidding? Who could sleep with all the excitement of the hurricane?"

"Hopefully, we've had the last of the exciting events for this storm."

"Are you going to sleep?"

He shook his head. "No." Exasperated and enchanted with her all at the same time, he gave in to the situation and leaned back against the edge of his desk. "I guess we should keep each other company while we wait it out."

He'd wanted it to be easier. He'd wanted her asleep so his libido would let him off the hook. But nothing about Annie ever seemed easy. Passionate, sensual and so full of life an aura of energy fairly shimmered around her.

"I've heard of hurricane parties. Maybe we could have one of those."

"Hmm. Depends on your idea of what would constitute a party."

"Well…there would be music. There's always music at a good party."

He smiled, despite himself. "If you haven't noticed, the only music you hear in this house comes from your CD player in the gym. And without electricity, retrieving that now would be useless."

"No music? My gosh, I hadn't realized." She stared up at him. "I can't imagine living in a house without music. At home, you could walk through the house and every room would have a different song playing. Don't you like music?"

"It isn't that," he confessed. "Growing up we didn't have much music in our house…aside from an occasional piano concerto played during a business reception."

"Your family had a piano and you didn't play it?"

He tried to keep the grimace off his face, but it was impossible. "I wanted to learn. But my father said piano playing would be of no use in business. I had the feeling he didn't think it was particularly masculine either."

Annie laughed. "Don't tell that to my brother Ryan. He plays every kind of music there is. Good enough that he can even take requests. And he's no sissy. He was a fullback on the Notre Dame football team. Now he's a fireman in Cambridge. He'd be a grand person to invite."

She'd been so animated as she talked about her brother. It was obvious that she loved her family. Her face glowed and she had bounced in her seat as she'd waved her hands throughout the story.

God, how he wanted her.

He would give up a month of his life to just once be able to capture that sexy mouth with his own. To run his hands through her fiery curls. To touch that smooth skin and finally bury himself deep inside her waiting warmth.

She was still driving him insane.

Waving a hand as if to dismiss the problem, she said, "Don't worry about the music. I can sing later if need be. What we really should have is beer or ale. That's another absolute necessity for a good Irish party."

"Sorry. I doubt that there's a beer in the house."

"Don't you like beer, either? My father would call

you a heretic." She laughed and the flashing green fire in her eyes made him too aware of her teasing.

"Be serious for once," he scowled. "Perhaps we should play a game of chess to pass the time."

"Don't know how to play. How about Hearts? I used to love to play that with my family."

"Hearts?"

"It's a card game."

He shrugged. "No playing cards in the house."

"Oh my gosh. A house with no playing cards and no beer. That's just sad."

He found himself laughing at his own expense. "You are absolutely impossible." But joking with her was turning him on even more than before. "I suppose in some ways I've been living in a dull world. At least it must seem that way to you," he managed.

"Oh I don't think your world is dull at all." She smiled and he felt his knees go weak. "Look around you. This is a fabulous mansion on an exotic Caribbean island. You can get on a jet and go anywhere in the world you want, any time you want. And in the meantime, you have a dolphin research facility where you can play with and talk to marine mammals. If that's not colorful, I don't know what is."

Through her eyes, the gray in his world faded away. It made him want more…more vibrancy…more life…more of Annie.

He loved to hear her talk. Just talk. Her voice had a lilt to it that rolled over him like warm honey.

"How about if we just talk to pass the time?" he asked, desperate to find something to take his mind off her body.

"Okay." She seemed to think that over a minute. "I know. We can tell stories."

"What kind of stories?"

"Ghost stories. With no electricity and all these shadows from the lanterns and candles jumping all over the room, ghost stories would be lots of fun."

He sat down on the sofa next to her. "I don't know any ghost stories."

"What? What kind of education have you had?" She chuckled and her eyes danced with delight.

Then she slid a glance over his shoulder and her whole demeanor suddenly changed. Her face drew up and her eyes grew dismal. Nick turned to see what had caught her attention and ruined her mood.

As he turned, he realized that she was staring at the picture of Christina. Hell.

He stood, grabbed the photo away from its spot on the table. "There are some ghost stories better left untold."

"Please don't move that because of me," she said sadly.

"Uh, I've been meaning to put it over behind my desk with the others of her." He stashed it, face-down, on the credenza in the darkest corner of the room. "She never cared much for that photograph anyway."

As he walked back to Annie's side, Nick noticed that she had tears in her eyes. Her expression was filled with sorrow and the tears welling there were poised to spill over her face.

"Annie?" He sat down on the sofa beside her again.

"I'm sorry." She fluttered her fingers in front of her as if to will away the tears. "It's just such a tragic love story. A young couple with so much to look forward to."

Nick couldn't stand to see the pain on Annie's face. Not when the truth of the tragedy was that there had been an absence of love. And he always felt better when Annie smiled. When she laughed, the whole world brightened.

A single drop leaked out of the corner of her eye. It tore a huge hole in him and he reached for her, rubbing a thumb under her eye to wipe her pain away with the tear.

"Annie, please…" He'd meant to say "please don't cry." At least, he thought that's what he'd meant.

But somewhere there, the entire mood in the room changed with one deep breath. He lifted her chin, leaned in and traced her full, rosy lips with his tongue. It was beyond him to stop.

Annie made a small sound and threw her arms around his neck to pull him closer and deepen the kiss. She was impossible to resist.

She was everything he'd ever wanted and had refused to let himself take. Though it made him mad to admit it, he knew that all his hard-won scruples and fidelity were just about to disappear into the night right along with his honor.

She moaned again. And a red haze of desire exploded in his head as he let Annie take him completely over the edge of reason.

Four

Annie went willingly, eagerly, into Nick's arms. Never before had she felt such power, nor such weakness.

Somewhere in the back of her mind, her mother's voice was telling her that this was wrong. Nick was her boss and they could never have any kind of future together. But…

Nick lathed her lips with his tongue, then nudged the lips open so he could sweep into her mouth. It gave her goose bumps but she tried her best to keep up with him.

Their tongues melded together and tangled as if in some erotic slow dance. Annie held her breath as he began to thrust his tongue forcefully back and forth into her mouth—demanding, enticing, begging.

He pulled back slightly, and buried his face in her neck on a deep breath. "I…I'm sorry," he stuttered against her skin. "I shouldn't. But I want you so much."

"I want you too," she readily agreed as she clung to his shoulders. The world suddenly turned blurry, hazy and the roar of the storm faded into a velvety blue buzz in her head. "Boy, do I ever."

On a groan, he nibbled his way up her throat as she threw back her head to give him access. He kissed her jawline, then moved to her ear. Taking the lobe in his mouth, he sucked gently then nipped with the lightest of bites. His warm breath tickled her ear.

Suddenly Annie saw stars.

"Oh my gosh. Is that the way this is supposed to feel? I know the novels say stuff about…um…" He slid his thumbs up over the tips of her breasts and she forgot the rest of her sentence—almost forgot her name.

But she did manage to remember that she didn't want him to guess about her total lack of experience. He might not want to keep going. And he just had to be the one.

She clamped her mouth shut. But when he reached under her T-shirt and tenderly stroked her breasts, she thought she might burst wide-open with erotic pulses.

Her clothes were all of a sudden too blessed tight. The T-shirt was choking her and the shorts were binding and making her sweat, especially between the thighs.

Nick dragged her to him and pulled her up into his lap. Wow. The feel of his manhood, pressed hard and solid against her bottom, gave her a jolt of courage. She grabbed the hem of her shirt and, with one swift tug, yanked it up and over her head.

The sudden cool draft of air against her heated skin

destroyed her newly found courage. Oh dear God. What had she done?

Nick's quick intake of breath told her he thought she had acted in haste, too. Too bold for her own good.

But when she made a move to cover her breasts with her hands, he grabbed her wrists and held them to her sides.

"Don't," Nick said with a rasp. "Don't cover yourself. You're so beautiful. Please. Please just let me look at you a minute."

Staring at her dusky, rose tips and the splash of brown freckles across her upper chest was causing a fresh blast of yearning to roll through Nick's body. This time it was so intense it flooded his gut and then gushed to his erection with such a compelling need that he could barely breathe.

She was such a kaleidoscope of life. He dropped her hands and let his own reach for what they saw—what they had desired for so long.

His fingers lightly touched her silken face while he watched those luminous emerald eyes turn sultry with passion. Shifting one hand to the back of her head, he grabbed a handful of curls and captured her fire. It was like liquid gold, spilling through his fingers.

Tentatively, Annie unbuttoned and pushed his shirt off his shoulders before reaching out to touch his bare chest. "You're pretty beautiful yourself. Or as they say in romance novels, 'a fine specimen of manhood.'"

When her hand connected with his skin, they both gasped as his heart thumped wildly in his chest. Her fingers began to draw lazy circles over the planes of his flesh and muscles. She dragged a nail over a nipple, then allowed her fingers to trail down his belly toward the waistband of his shorts.

He blinked his eyes against the aroused heat and thickness in his body. Swallowing hard, he knew he had to keep his eyes open, to see clearly what he could make her body do. His fingers lingered against the smooth satin of her neck, then inched lower to the shallow indentation at the base.

Watching her face closely for any sign of distress, he saw that her lips parted slightly as he lowered his hand to cup one breast. It fit perfectly into his palm, so once more he gingerly moved his thumb over the tip. And this time he was able to watch it peak for him.

Annie closed her eyes and took a breath, as if the feel of his hands on her skin was the most exquisite thing that had ever happened to her. She arched her back, urging him ever closer.

Just one taste. Someplace in the back of his mind, he knew this must stop. But first he had to experience all that striking energy—how it would taste—how it would feel against the flat of his tongue.

She looked up at him with heavy-lidded eyes. "Nick, please…"

The sound of his name, drew him up and he swore softly. "This is a huge mistake," he growled as he dropped his hands. He let her slide off his lap and began to inch away from her.

"No." She took his hand, put it back to her breast and held it there with her own. "Please touch me. Kiss me. Make love with me."

The look on her face ran a shudder of desire through

his body as he struggled to be fair—to someone. But he wasn't exactly sure who. He just had to be sure the situation was something Annie understood.

"I have nothing to offer you but…this one night," he told her in a rough voice. "I can't give you…I can't give anyone…"

"I know," she said softly. "It's okay. I understand." She smiled with that devastating need, shining clear and transparent in her eyes—and he was totally lost.

He braced a hand on the sofa and touched her face with the other as he leaned in for another kiss. She tasted so good, just the way she looked. Like red cherry and chocolate candy. Like being caught up in a whirlwind of color and magic.

Dizzy, he slid off the sofa and knelt before her but never broke the kiss. She was so tiny that he could reach her better from this position. With his knees sinking into the thick oriental rug below them, he forgot all about the storm outside and concentrated instead on capturing the storm of her desire.

Annie put her arms around his shoulders and pulled him to her, pressing her naked breasts to his chest. The quiver of need was like nothing she had ever felt before. She rubbed her tender nipples back and forth against the smattering of hair and held her breath.

Intense bolts of pleasure moved downward from her breasts, landing with a surprise of tingles way deep inside her. She could have sworn she felt those zesty bubbles all the way down in that secret spot between her legs, though it didn't seem possible.

She heard herself moan and vaguely wondered if

she should be quiet. Do nothing to ruin the mood or make him change his mind.

A small and fleeting thought about the possibility of getting pregnant chased through her mind. But then she remembered that he'd said that he and his wife had tried and couldn't.

That thought depressed her again. But when Nick began to nibble his way down her neck and chest, she totally forgot everything but the sensations he was creating across her skin and deep within her body.

He rubbed his hands up and down her spine as he tasted and sucked first one nipple then the other.

"Nick," she groaned. "Wait. Let me touch you, too."

He pulled his head up and gazed into her blazing green eyes, full of passion and want. Holding on to her shoulders so he wouldn't spin right off the planet, he let her run her palms across his face, neck and chest. As she touched and explored, her expression became dazed, her eyes glazed over.

His breathing became ever more ragged. Thunder began to build in his head and split through his blood. A roar of passion to replace the noise of the storm outside. But he resolved to let this passionate leprechaun do as she wished. Just so long as she allowed him to watch as the pleasure ran across her expressive face.

He watched as her skin flushed a rosy shade of pink. The blush moved across her chest, and on up her neck to her cheeks. Flaming her. Burning him with desire.

Patience, he cautioned himself. It had been so long, and she was more wonderful than he'd thought possible.

Make it last.

It had been two years since he'd so much as touched a woman. But even back then he had not needed Christine this desperately. He wanted to experience everything with Annie, every second of the fire that was all-consuming.

She moved her hands up his neck then touched his chin, his forehead, his eyelids. As if she too wanted this to last, and was trying to memorize every inch of him.

Her eyes were aflame, blazing emerald with irises black with passion. He glanced down her body and saw the dusky nipples darken to deepest purple as the blood pulsed through her. It made him wonder what other parts of her might be darkening as they engorged with blood and fire.

He gave himself permission to touch her at will, to flick a nail over her extended tips. To run his hands up and down her rib cage and capture her breasts in his palms, weighing them and cherishing them. She fit his hands exactly.

The weird sensation of being made for each other, of somehow finding the other half of him, made him sway into her. He nipped her lips with a light touch. She moaned and dug her nails into his shoulders, dragging him to her and deepening the kiss.

The sweetness of her mouth combined with the sweet pain of her nails on his skin, drove his sex further into arousal. He pushed her backward on the sofa, gasping and groaning like an animal.

Running his hands down her sides, he ripped her shorts from her body with one swift tug. She lay naked before him, an intense and luxuriant goddess with a glazed expression.

He wanted to touch her everywhere. Taste her everywhere. The hunger was fierce inside him, driving him to do things he'd never done.

Burying his face in her abdomen, he circled her belly button with his tongue. Her skin was smooth, silky, like the glide of expensive brandy down his throat.

Moving lower, he licked a path toward the ginger colored curls at the apex of her thighs. As he stole a taste of her, he glanced back up to her face and saw the pleasure she was feeling written clearly there.

The hues of her were spectacular. Reds of desire, and hazy deep purples of need.

Nick wanted to give in to her every wish, just as she was giving him everything he had ever wanted. Everything he could ever imagine.

Touching her nub with the edge of his tongue, Nick lifted her hips then slid a finger into her warm, wet depths. Annie moaned and writhed her hips. She drove her hands into his hair in a violent rage.

He knew the feeling well. His own resolve to go slow faltered and fell by the wayside as he stood, dragging his running shorts down and off with one quick flick of his wrist. He could manage no more.

He paused a second to draw a breath and looked down at Annie, her eyes were round, her lips parted. She made a tiny mewling noise and reached out to touch his rigid sex.

Annie tentatively ran a finger up his shaft, blinking at the moisture she found at the tip. He groaned and pulled her hand away, afraid he would embarrass himself beyond redemption if he didn't have her now. Right now.

Urging her to lay lengthwise on the sofa, he fit himself between her legs. Not breathing and not thinking, he lowered himself to his elbows and took her face in his hands as his sex nudged her waiting warmth.

Her hands moved over his back and she arched, silently pleading with him to take her higher. He was more than ready to oblige.

He caught her buttocks in one hand and prepared to fit himself within her depths as he lifted her body up to meet his. It was a slow and agonizingly pleasurable venture inside her waiting warmth. So good. So right.

He groaned and he let himself inch deeper. Wanting this to be good for her, he stopped with only his tip buried where he was dying to follow. He wanted to give her a moment to adjust to his size. She was tight, warm, wet. Ready.

Annie stilled under him and for a moment he thought that's what she was doing, judging his fit, allowing the pleasure to wash over and through her. Then he went a millimeter deeper and felt the resistance, heard her intake of breath.

"Annie? My God. You're not…" He was stunned and puzzled. All this passion and erotic color lying under him. She couldn't be…

"Please don't stop, Nick. Please." The agonizing plea in her voice, the desperate need so clear in her words, probably wouldn't have been enough to drive him over the edge and do something that was so wrong.

But she planted her feet on either side of his hips, gripped him and arched upward. Hard. Hard enough to drive him past all resistance and impale him deep inside her body.

She breathed a relieved sigh. "Thank heaven. Hurry, Nick. Please hurry."

And in that instant, he was gone. All he could see, all he could hear, all he could feel was her glorious heat, surrounding him and gripping him with overwhelming desire.

She was sobbing under him, begging innocently with her body for something she couldn't know. He bent his neck and sucked her nipple into his mouth as he fought to show her.

When her body began to shudder around him, Annie moaned with a low, keening cry that sounded like it had been ripped from her body. She dug her nails into his back and bit his shoulder as the shock waves rolled over them both.

Once again, in the deep recesses of his mind, the feeling that everything was exactly the way it should be slid in and out of his consciousness.

Nick shoved the strange feeling aside and gave way to the rippling pull of passion. He thrust into her with a violent and mindless madness until he too felt waves of frantic release. Grasping her tightly to him, he let the power and the magic roll over them as they flew high above the storm—high above reality—and rode the lightning bolts safe in each others arms.

Reality returned to Annie in stages. Euphoria and boneless giddiness came first as Nick kissed her senseless. Their breathing was erratic. Their legs and arms still intimately entwined.

Wow. Oh wow. So this was what her sisters had raved about. No, couldn't be. This was so much better than any description she'd ever heard or read. She was dazzled.

Finally, Nick lifted his upper body, leaned on his elbows and cradled her head between his huge hands. "Are you all right?" His eyes were glazed, his expression rather foggy, but his first thought was for her welfare.

"Wonderful. How about you?" To her ears, that shaky whisper had come out sounding more like a purr. Small wonder. She felt as contented as a well-fed kitten.

His eyes smiled while he placed tiny kisses all over her face. On her eyelids, her chin, her temple. Nick was adoring her, cherishing her with his lips. The kisses were such intimate gestures that she nearly cried from the beauty of them.

"I'm dizzy with wanting you. Again." He shifted his hips, pulling free. But she still felt the power in his lower body as it pressed hard against hers. "And again."

Annie reached her arms as far around his waist as they would go and squeezed him tightly to her. "Sounds good to me." She could stay here with him like this forever.

Touching his lips lightly to hers, he groaned against them. "You are so free. God, you're generous and…exquisite."

She wiggled her bottom and got another groan for her trouble.

He raised his head again to gaze into her eyes. "But any more tonight would be too much for your first time. You were a virgin, Annie. Why didn't you say something?"

"I didn't want to spoil it," she admitted. "I wanted you. Everything else was not important."

"It's important to me. I needed you so badly tonight, but I shouldn't have been the one."

"Why? You have just given me the most wonderful gift of my entire lifetime," she whispered. "You're like the best Christmas present. The ultimate favor I've wanted my whole life and never had the courage to go out and ask for. Please don't make it sound bad."

Nick made a strangled sound deep in his throat and one of his hands strayed to her breast. As he teased the nipple, he gazed deep into her eyes.

It appeared to her as though he was trying to see into her soul. Finally, he bent his head and licked a path across her chest and down to the other sensitized breast.

Annie felt the heat explode through her, sending shock waves of pleasure that punctuated her need and enlarged it with his every movement.

She decided to take her own destiny into her hands for one of the very few times in her life. At last she was grown-up enough to know what she wanted and how to go get it. And what she wanted was more of Nick.

"You know, I'm very athletic and healthy," she murmured in his ear with a small moan. "I don't think it would hurt me any to try that again now. Right now. Please." She bumped her hips against his groin.

"That's cheating, Annie." But as he said the words one of his hands slipped between them, moved to the juncture of her thighs and lightly stroked and cupped, bringing dampness and moisture into his hand.

"No…" she insisted against his shoulder. "That's asking for what I want."

She bit into his neck and Nick groaned as she felt a shudder move through him. He eased his shaft inside her body again and waited, as if he wanted her to be sure.

She was more sure of him…of this night…than anything before. She lifted her hips as much as possible and sighed with the relief of having him deep inside once more. It felt strangely right, strangely familiar.

He began moving, slowly this time. Back and forth. Slow and sure. Nick was drawing her up, one agonizing inch at a time, as his lips moved over her skin. Kissing her shoulders, lips, breasts, he was building the fire between them to daredevil heights.

She squirmed, and this time when Annie burst into flames, they were all-consuming, all-absorbing. As her body began to let go, she felt him trembling, relenting, rippling with pleasure right along beside her.

Nick gripped her so tightly that she felt safe enough to fall over any edge with him. Wild explosions rocked through them both. She screamed at the exact moment Nick threw back his head and cried out to the heavens.

The world tilted. The storm thrashed wildly about them. And crazy images of forever burst into Annie's soul.

Five

It must be a true magical spell that could fill the night with such enchantment, Annie thought. She leaned up on one hand and rested her back against the sofa, staring down at Nick as he dozed next to her.

He was absolutely *the* most gorgeous man. She loved his aristocratic features. The high cheekbones and sculpted jawline were a perfect match for his broad shoulders and long muscular limbs. She also found especially endearing the steel-blue hue that his eyes became whenever she caught him watching her.

Annie used the tip of her finger to trace the frown lines across his forehead. Soon she felt a corresponding but vague frown in the vicinity of her heart.

It wasn't particularly flattering for him to be having a bad dream right after making love with her. She fervently hoped his nightmare wasn't caused by anything she'd done.

But she had to guess that this dream was probably caused by the memory of his lost wife. Nick's mother had told her that his wife had died in the same yachting accident that blew out his knee. She'd also said that Nick had tried to save his wife, nearly drowning himself in the attempt.

Annie imagined that he must dwell on the accident. Maybe that was why he became so irritable on occasion.

Whenever Annie knew that Nick's body was causing him pain, she also clearly saw the ache of a bad memory in his eyes. Occasionally, she'd even caught a hint of guilt hiding behind that pain.

The minute she thought of his guilt, it made her uncomfortable. The idea of Nick having either pain or guilt over his wife's death so soon after the two of them had been intimate together made her totally miserable.

Not the least bit sorry she'd made love to this beautiful but haunted man, Annie nevertheless found herself falling into a depression. After finally finding such fabulous power and need, it was with a man who would never be free from his memories.

Sometimes life really did suck and then you died— just exactly like the joke her brother-in-law taught her.

But how fantastic it was to have captured that power, even if just for a few minutes. A vision ran through her head of how it had been. Of having his mouth on hers. Of the warmth and tenderness of his touch, and of the flames in his eyes when he gazed at her naked body.

"Oh, dear Lord," she softly groaned aloud. The end-ing of this fairy-tale romance was not going to be a happily ever after.

The two of them surely must have been under some sort of spell tonight. But thank heaven for it. Otherwise she would never have known…

She gazed down at his long silver lashes, spilling over his cheeks as he slumbered beside her. In her soul, she knew he was going to eventually regret what they'd done.

Making love to her boss had definitely been wrong. But she'd wanted him so badly. Now all she wanted was for him to allow her to continue to be his assistant. She wasn't sure she could bear it if he sent her away now. Not before she made sure he was healthy and settled in his new life.

Nick had to care a little about her, he'd made that clear enough. Perhaps she could figure out how to make him want to keep her with him for a while longer. Maybe just until she could think about losing him forever without having this horrible ache in her heart.

Fighting off the pain, she gently flipped a lock of his hair back off his forehead. Such soft hair, so smooth and silky. She swallowed the tears that threatened.

"Hello, beautiful," he said as he lifted heavy eyelids to look at her. "You doing all right?"

She nodded, but could find no words as he rubbed a warm palm up her arm. Heat and desire were still in his eyes. She was so glad not to see regret in them yet, that it was all she could do not to sob openly with relief.

"That was amazing," he murmured. "You're amazing."

The tears escaped, falling against her will.

"Hey. What's wrong? I didn't hurt you, did I?"

Shaking her head, she blinked hard and took a breath. "Certainly not. It's just that…we're going to regret this after the storm is over, aren't we?"

"Come here, Annie. Just let me hold you a second." He wrapped her up in his arms and placed tiny, whispered kisses against her hair. "I will never regret one second of my time with you. And I would hope that we can grow closer because of what's been between us, not more distant.

"After the storm, we can still work together," he continued with a soft sigh. "But we'll be friends who've shared something special. Simple, right?"

The words didn't feel right to her. There was something about what he'd said that seemed wrongheaded. The very idea of it sounded too easy, and she worried that nothing about how she felt now could ever be classified as simple.

But Annie wouldn't tell him no. She was sure she could *never* say no to this wonderful man.

"Okay, I guess. Sure," she said against his chest. It was so safe and warm here, she might've agreed to anything just to be able to stay exactly like this—in the heat and glory of his arms.

"Great. Now then…" He began to unwrap his arms from around her as he dragged them both up to sitting positions.

"The storm can't be over yet," she whined and clung to him. "I can still hear the rain on the shutters."

Nick glanced at her face as the candlelight danced over her skin. He let his gaze drop to her naked chest where her nipples stood peaked and high. "Um…no, not yet. But I sort of thought you might need time. I still believe you're going to be sore after your first experience—and I was getting hungry. But…"

Nick grabbed her up and tumbled them both to the rug, loving the way she'd gasped then sighed as he clamped his mouth on hers. Letting his fingers glide down the satin of her skin, he touched the inside of her thighs and smiled against her lips when he heard the moan coming from deep within her chest.

If he didn't touch her everywhere, taste her everywhere again right this minute, he would surely die. All of a sudden, Nick found himself hoping the storm would rage on forever.

"I can't hear the winds or the rain anymore," Annie whispered.

Nick squeezed her hand, flicked the flashlight beam around at the darkened hallway and continued to creep slowly onward toward the kitchen. Heaven only knew how many hours it had been since the storm had begun to unleash its fury over the island. He'd been too pleasantly occupied to pay much attention.

"I'll try to tune in the weather channel on the battery-powered shortwave radio in the kitchen," he told her. "Just as soon as we get something to eat. I'm starved."

"No kidding," she laughed and waved a hand toward both their bare bodies. "We were hungry enough to sneak into the kitchen without even stopping to get dressed. I just hope no one walks in on us."

"Not to worry. Everyone left on the island knows enough to stay put until the storm is really over." He led them into the wide, industrial kitchen area and dropped her hand so he could light a couple of lamps that he knew were stashed in a cupboard.

As soon as the glow illuminated the way, Annie pulled plates and glasses from their spots in the butler's pantry. She set about fixing them both a hot meal on the propane stove.

Nick sat back and watched her work. She looked like a pixie with curls bouncing, energy bubbling off her naked body and eyes concentrating hard on her cooking. So young, he thought. So untouched by trouble in her short life.

It reminded him of his own life's tragedies, and the thought brought his usual automatic irritation to the surface for a moment. But when Annie turned to him and smiled, it felt like nothing could ever be wrong in the world again.

"Do you think the water will be okay to drink after the storm?" she asked as she popped the tops on two bottled waters.

"We're supplied by cisterns and they should be fine. It may be a problem getting the water out of the pipes without electricity to run the pumps, though. But as soon as we're sure the storm has run its course, I'll go start up the emergency generators."

"Wonderful. That'll mean we can have hot water too, won't it?" She carried their plates to the table and sat down beside him.

"Yes. Are you thinking of a shower, or the dishes?" The minute he'd mentioned it, Nick had thought about making love to her under the shower spray.

She grinned at him. "Both."

With the two of them still nude, it surprised him how

free and easy she was in her body. Christina would never have wandered around the house without clothes.

He waited for that thought to make him feel the old annoyance that always accompanied the pain, but it didn't come. Perhaps if he dwelt on it for long enough it might. But he would much rather dwell on the way the sight of Annie's body caused a sense of deepening arousal to move through his blood. Would he never tire of wanting her?

He noticed that Annie's mouth was still swollen from their kisses and wondered if his was the same. Studying her neck and shoulders while she ate a spoonful of stew, he saw that they carried the marks of their love-making.

All the things they'd done flooded back in a rush of lurid and sensual detail. The two of them had acted like animals. Untamed. Wild.

Like nothing in his experience.

But looking at her now, it appeared incongruent. Her young innocent face versus the marks of passion on her neck. A niggle of guilt seeped into his conscious mind. He had seduced a virgin and he hadn't even been drunk.

Worse, the virgin was also the woman who had come to mean so much to him over the past few months. The woman who had been more than compassionate and patient while she retrained his muscles. The woman who had taught him to laugh again.

When she'd asked about regrets earlier, the mere thought that she might not stay by his side had caused him to panic and reach for her again. It might be too much to hope that she would stay his personal trainer forever. After all, he had nearly all his mobility and strength back. Someday soon he would be completely healed and she would go.

But he was determined to think of a way to keep her with him just a little longer. He vowed to find every respectable reason to keep her on the island for as long as physically possible. If not in his bed, at least near enough that he could be sure she was okay.

And in the meantime… He grabbed her free hand, turned it over and placed a whispered kiss into her palm. They still had time. The storm wasn't over yet.

The hurricane rains had died down hours ago, and Annie's mind was filling with regrets once again.

She swung her legs over the edge of the sofa in Nick's office and set her teacup down next to her empty bread plate on the side table. Everything had been so free and easy while the storm raged on. What would happen now that it had passed over them?

The idea that they would have each other for however long the storm continued had sounded good last night. She'd thought afterwards they might be able to go back to the way it was before. Now, however, everything looked different.

Annie was achy all over. Interesting muscles she'd forgotten she had were shrieking in protest. Still, if Nick reached for her again right now, she'd jump him without so much as a second thought.

Unfortunately, he wasn't here. He'd gone outside to start up the generators and check for damage. He'd said he wouldn't try to go down to the dolphin lagoon until he could be sure the house was not in danger of collapse.

She found her shorts and top in a heap behind the sofa and slipped them on. Wondering absently what she would do if she couldn't find a way to make him want her to stay on the island, she moved over to the wide office desk and sat in his huge armchair, trying to comfort herself.

It made her feel like a doll, sitting at his desk. But the chair smelled of him. All leather and musk and masculine scent.

Her back was to the pictures of his wife and she wanted to will them out of her life forever. No, that wouldn't be right. Nick had loved his wife once and she had died. Annie couldn't hate a dead woman who had no more choices left. Their story was such a tragedy.

Annie had wondered if the intense attraction she knew Nick felt for her would be enough to help him overcome some of his old pain so he could find a new life. She'd wanted to help him capture a little bit of happiness again. And if that happiness could be with her, well, all the better.

Sighing, Annie had to admit she had no training in psychology and no way to help him get over his pain and guilt. Life seldom turned out like it did in novels.

Running her gaze over his clean desktop to keep her thoughts from becoming overwhelming, she wasn't the least surprised at how neat he was. Papers were stacked and filed in proper folders. Nothing was out of place or messy. But it also appeared to be rather somber and isolated—just like the man who lived and worked here.

Something shiny at the edge of the desk stood out from the rest and caught her attention. She reached for it and discovered it was a book with a heavy gold-and-ivory cover.

This must be the magic book Nick had mentioned yesterday. Annie ran her fingers over the inlaid ivory and closed her eyes. Yes, with her eyes shut she could definitely feel a special vibration there. Maybe the book was indeed filled with magic.

She started to open it, to see what sorcery the pages might contain. But Nick came into the office just in that instant.

"Water should be hot enough for a shower in a few minutes," he said with a smile.

Annie set the book down and jumped up. "Is the storm over then?"

"The winds are still gusting past gale force, according to the weather channel. I'd better wait another couple of hours before going down the beach to the lagoon."

"I'm sure the dolphins will be okay. You have the very best people working with them."

He leaned over and gave her a quick hug. "I only hire the very best." He stepped away but kept a hand on her shoulder. "I'm going back out to try stabilizing the roof on the new wing. It shouldn't take too long."

Once again searching his handsome face and darkened blue eyes for any sign of regrets, she was pleased to see instead that desire still flamed in them. Passion rippled pleasure across his features. Passion for her. What a high it gave her to know he wanted her as much as she wanted him.

Pulling her to his chest, Nick kissed her fast and hard. She nearly fainted from the sensation it caused in her gut.

Thank heaven for the winds. She still had a little time to figure out how to put off facing their ultimate destiny.

Annie tried to clear her mind but standing under the vibrating water jets in Nick's shower stall was fogging up her senses. The bewitched night with him had been beyond her wildest imaginings. But she knew the storm, and their time together, was almost over.

Everything between them had changed.

Would he allow her to continue working with him—to help him? Deathly afraid that her emotions were going to get in the way, she worried that maybe the two of them had to talk about it anyway.

But for now, stinging needles of pulsing water sent hot messages to every body part, reminding her of Nick's touch…of his kisses. If she closed her eyes, she could imagine the water was his fingers, caressing and stirring her body to life.

She began to ache for him again.

The glass shower door behind her snapped open and she spun around to find Nick, stepping naked into the shower. "What are you doing?" she squealed with a laugh.

"The winds have picked up once again. The hurricane's not over. We've been given more time."

He reached for her, dragging her into his embrace and kissing her senseless. Not that her senses were overly sharp right this minute. Her whole world had become hazy, soft and all watery around the edges.

Along with her body. Her knees wobbled as he slid his hard slick chest against hers.

Annie grabbed hold of his upper arms to steady herself, but Nick didn't give her a chance to fall. He lifted her off her feet and encouraged her to wrap her legs around his waist.

He turned them both around and pressed her back against the shower wall. The water pounded down on them while he entered her with one swift and sure thrust.

"I couldn't stay away when I heard the water running and knew you were in here—naked," he groaned. "I needed… I shouldn't have…"

Whatever else he had wanted to say was lost to the heat and the fire they created. By now, Annie thought she should be too familiar with his body inside hers to be surprised by the explosions he caused.

But each time was a shock of electricity, warmth and blinding passion. They rocked violently, but in perfect harmony, under the beat and sting of the water all around them.

Together they left the world, their reality and the ticking clock of the time they had left far, far behind.

An hour later, they sat dressed in shorts and T-shirts at the kitchen table. Annie bit into a banana that she'd just peeled, and Nick's mouth watered. The image of her wrapping those wide, full lips around certain body parts of his made him instantly hard again.

This had to stop. The winds had finally died down for good and he needed to get back to business. He had to stop driving himself crazy wanting her.

And they had to come to some agreement about their future. As soon as everyone returned to the island, things would get back to normal.

But everything seemed so different now. He felt a core change in himself since making love to Annie. Not able to think clearly about it, Nick brushed aside the strange new sensations.

He would dig up his old reserve and put distance back between them. She would hopefully agree to continue being his trainer. Perhaps this would even turn out to be his second chance in life for friendship. Maybe that's what these strange feelings were trying to tell him.

Friendship would be wonderful, but every time Annie gazed up at him, he felt the heat in her eyes. That would complicate things. He was not "forever" material. He'd already proven that with one desolate marriage. He was not about to drag Annie down, too.

This crazy storm brought them together, but it had just been wild sex. He'd better find his missing self-control. And fast.

It was bad enough that he'd broken the promise to himself about celibacy. Hmm. On second thought, that was one promise he was extremely glad he'd broken.

But never again.

He intended to talk to Annie. Perhaps if he explained everything just right, she would agree to remain on the island and become his friend.

There was no way he could bear to lose her entirely. The mere thought of never seeing her again drove an icy wedge of pain deep into his chest.

"Listen," Annie said, bringing him out of his thoughts. "I think I hear someone calling you."

Both he and Annie stood and moved toward the hallway. But before he got to the doorway, Rob Bellamy appeared and moved into the kitchen toward them. Rob was the ex-SEAL who had stayed to look after the dolphins.

"You two make it through the storm in one piece?" Rob asked.

"We're fine. But I can't say as much for sections of the roof. How'd the dolphins come through?"

"We made it okay during most of the storm," Rob answered. "But just when it looked like we were home free, there was one last storm surge that tore a hole in the perimeter fencing. Two of the dolphins came up for breath right then and were caught up in the outflow."

It was all Nick could do to keep from panicking. He snapped his mouth shut for fear of saying something he would regret and paced to the sink and back again.

"Which two?" Annie asked Rob. "Not Sultana."

Rob nodded and Nick fisted his hands. "Where are they? Did you call them back with the sound transmitters?"

"We have them back in the lagoon now. They didn't want to be outside any more than we wanted them to be. But the shock of it distressed them both."

"Sultana?"

"She's gone into early labor. That's why I'm here. We could sure use an extra pair of hands in the lagoon."

"Go back down there," Nick ordered. "I'll put on shoes and follow right behind you."

Rob left and Nick turned to Annie. "Stay here. You'll be safe. I'll try to call you later if the phone service comes back up."

"No," she said and delayed him by laying a hand on his arm. "I'm coming with you."

He shook his head, but she tightened her grip on his arm. "I don't need protecting, Nick. I'm more capable than you are of helping in the lagoon. You haven't been in the water since…you know."

She had him there. If it came down to who was the stronger swimmer, he would lose. In the excitement he'd forgotten his hesitation about returning to the ocean.

"All right, fine," he muttered.

But he had a strange feeling that nothing was ever going to be fine between the two of them again.

Nick sat on his haunches and braced his hands against the edge of the wooden deck that spanned the lagoon. He held his breath as he watched the three humans and one mother dolphin labor, trying to bring a new life into the world early.

Rob and Elinor Stansky both had on scuba gear and periodically each would surface to give instructions to Annie. Nick was stiff from holding himself rigid. His nerves were shot.

But Annie was a marvel of serene determination as she half swam and half walked through the choppy water. She kept up a steady stream of chatter directed toward Sultana; soothing, settling and calming the distraught mother-to-be.

When Nick caught a glimpse of Annie's eyes, he saw they were shining and bright with breathless awe. She was experiencing a new high, a glimpse of nature's wonder.

It made him ache, thinking that it should be Christina there in the lagoon with her beloved dolphin. She would've killed to have this opportunity to bring one to life.

Of all the things Nick wished that he could've done for Christina, bringing babies into the world was number one on his list. Any baby.

He didn't consider himself a superstitious man, but he sensed that there was some preordained reason why Annie was the one here and very much alive. She was so different. Not as sophisticated as Christina, and not as technically pretty either, she was so much more vivid and full of energy.

He'd already idly wondered about what advancing age would bring to Annie's features. Imagining that her colors would soften, Nick just knew her face would grow more round and beautiful with every year. In his mind, he could even see the tiny, laugh lines as they grew bolder around her eyes.

Nick refused to think about the very strong probability that he would never get the chance to know how she would look then. Would never be able to grow old with her.

For now, Annie was as wild and free as a dolphin. She was strong and special. And he wanted her again so badly he was nearing explosion.

Nick bit back his inappropriate needs and Sultana's baby was soon delivered. Laughing and clapping her hands, Annie bounced out of the lagoon and ran toward him.

Her hair was damp, her green eyes dancing.

And Nick vowed they would have their talk about being just friends. They would—just as soon as he saw those big eyes darken while he slid inside her—one more time.

Six

The next couple of days—and nights—went by in a blur of activity. It was as if a steamy romance novel and a fairy-tale life had magically combined to make Annie happier than she'd ever been.

While Nick worked with a crew from the village, cleaning up the air-landing strip and bringing back the islands's electric power, she helped out in the lagoon and kept the center's records straight for him. No one had been able to leave or return to the island yet and a wonderful sense of community had developed within the small survivor's group.

"That's enough," she told Nick as he finished his last rep with the barbells. "It's almost dawn. Let's go get something to eat." She threw him a towel, laughing when it hit him in the head.

He cocked an eyebrow and before she could move

away from him, he had her in his arms. His hands were everywhere all at once as he kissed and tickled, ruffled and stirred.

"Nick! We're all sweaty. Stop that," she chuckled.

Groaning, he grabbed her bottom with both hands and dragged her up against his groin. "Sex is best when it's messy," he whispered in her ear.

She sighed and clung to him. It was a major miracle that she'd learned enough about sensual things over the past few days to agree with him about that.

Her breathing became ragged, and the stars that a few minutes ago had disappeared from the early-morning heavens were suddenly back. But this time they were in her eyes. Nick could make her lose her mind and become blind with need by just a touch.

"I can't seem to keep my hands off of you," he moaned. But a minute later he pulled away and dropped his hands after he'd made sure she was steady on her feet. "I think we'd better stop now, though. Let's go to the kitchen for breakfast."

After they'd eaten fruit and bread and had coffee, Nick asked that she accompany him to his office. She'd noticed a quiet, sobering change in him during the last few minutes of breakfast. And when she smiled and raised and lowered her eyebrows suggestively, he only shook his head.

"Afraid we don't have time this morning, Annie," he told her harshly. "We need to talk."

Heaven help her. She'd wondered when the "talk" would happen. But she didn't feel ready quite yet. Wanting just one more day, one more hour, even a few more minutes in his arms, she tried again to search his eyes for that soft blue haze of desire she loved seeing so much. But it wasn't there.

Nick was all business as he led them to the office. He motioned for her to sit at his desk instead of on the sofa. Then he perched his bottom on the edge of the desk next to her. Too close to ignore, yet too distant to touch.

"We have the airstrip back in good enough shape so that the first of the returning staff will be able to fly in from the States later this morning," he said softly. "I intend to be aboard the plane for its round trip out."

"Oh?" Annie wondered if that meant he wanted her to go along. Maybe this was his way of sending her back to the States and firing her.

She took a breath and asked. "Will you need me with you when you go?" If this was the end, she intended to leave gracefully.

"I need you to stay here," he said.

Taking another deep breath because she found she'd been holding the last one, Annie straightened her spine and waited for the rest. She refused to cry, dammit.

"I'd like for you to take over my responsibilities with the research center," he said roughly. "Working with the scientists in the lagoon and doing the paperwork. Just more of the things you've been taking care of for the last few days. Would you mind?"

Stunned, she fought not to let her voice give away how badly he'd gotten to her. "Mind? Not at all. Personal trainers have to keep records on their clients that are quite similar. And I love working with dolphins. But why won't you be doing it?"

Nick took a deep breath himself, as if he'd been

afraid of her answer. "When I return to the island, I'll
be bringing construction crews and equipment with me.
There's so much destruction from the storm. The village is in shambles. Houses, businesses, even the clinic
has been partially destroyed. It'll take us a couple of
months of hard work to get things back in order."

She'd only been traveling to the lagoon and back to
this house since the day of the storm. But the way he
described the island, it sounded awful. Except of course,
the part about her staying here to help him out with the
research center.

Nick narrowed his gaze at her. "There's something
else. Uh…about us."

Well, finally. Here came the part she'd known they
had to get to eventually. She bit her lip to keep in the
scream that was threatening to overwhelm her.

But before Nick could say what he'd meant, a sudden
gust of her nasty pride reared its square little chin, causing her mouth to open and words to come spilling out
without thought. "You don't have to tell me, I know, your
knee is healed. I've been trying to think of a way to tell
you it was time for me to go anyway. This'll be a good opportunity for us to make the break and yet still allow me
to continue to help out on the island I've grown to love."

The frown lines appeared on his forehead, but he
crossed his arms over his chest and didn't say anything.

Inside she was crying, but outside she managed a half
smile and hurried ahead—with words spewing and
thoughts flying. "Thank you for being kind enough
to…uh…show me the ropes during the storm, so to
speak. I'll be forever grateful and I just know we'll be
the dearest friends until our dying days.

"You were so right when you said it would be simple. Our hormones were just acting up because of the storm." She babbled on, afraid that if she stopped it would be on a sob.

"If you'll just help me gather up my things from the ruins of my suite before you go, I'll move out to the pool house while you're in the States. I realize your mother likes to stay out there when she comes to visit, but there should be room for us both in the two bedrooms and it will be so much more…respectable that way when the staff returns."

She gulped in a breath and started for the door. "Let's go grab a shower and meet back here in an hour. Okay?"

Annie almost made the doorway before she realized what she'd just said and spun back to him. "I mean…we'll each grab a shower…separately. And get dressed…in different rooms."

Nick was still scowling, but he never made a move or a sound. So she turned around and literally ran out of the door before she made a total fool of herself and begged for him to come with her—one last time.

She knew she had lots of crying and damning of the saints to do. And it would be much better if she got a good head start on that while in the shower. All alone.

Passionata grew agitated as she gazed into the crystal. The fog of time covered her view as she turned away, shaking her head and softly cursing.

"Wrong direction, young Scoville. All wrong."

Crossing arms under her breasts, she let her lips narrow into a disapproving line. "I'd hoped this would be easier. But no…

"Stubborn man." She frowned. "All right. It is past time to stir in trouble, make you reach out for solutions. Let's just see how bad we can make your circumstances before you give in to the magic."

She waved a hand over her crystal and invoked the magic. "Every difficult travail will come your way now, Scoville. Remember the magic. Use it at long last."

"Most of the reconstruction is completed then?" Nick's mother asked him over the phone early one morning.

It had been six weeks since the hurricane and he'd been working eighteen hour days trying to get the village back in shape. He hadn't minded the hard work a bit. Most of the time it kept him busy enough so that his mind didn't wander back to Annie.

Nick had moved his office down to a construction shack near the village and turned his own in the main house over to Annie so she could keep the dolphin records in his place. The few times they'd been in each other's company since the storm had been totally unsatisfactory and had left him aching and miserable.

There had been those two conflicted and terribly quiet meals they had shared on the nights when he just couldn't bear to think of her eating alone. And their extremely short biweekly meetings to discuss the dolphin center had been stilted and more than a little uncomfortable.

But other than those wonderful yet miserable times, he'd done a good job of pretending to avoid her.

Except, of course, for when he'd snuck down to watch her work in the lagoon without letting anyone spot him. He could scarcely believe he'd turned into some kind of damned pervert, watching her and wanting her. And never letting Annie know about it.

Staying away from her was in her best interest, though. And he'd promised himself from the moment she'd moved out of the main house that he would always consider her interests first. Always. No matter what it cost him.

"Nicholas?" his mother's voice broke into his thoughts. "Are you feeling all right? I'm quite positive you've been getting enough rest and haven't been working too hard because I know Annie would never allow that."

"I'm fine, Mother. A little tired maybe." He hadn't been sleeping well at all. His dreams and thoughts kept centering around Annie and wondering what she was doing. And on what he would like to be doing with her.

"Annie's been busy with the dolphins," he continued without giving it enough thought first. "We haven't seen much of each other since the storm."

His mother made a distressed noise into the phone and urged him to pay more attention to Annie and her instructions. He found his mother's words terribly annoying. She really had no need to tell him how wonderful Annie was. He probably knew it better than anyone else on earth.

But that didn't make it right for him to be with Annie…to use her just to satisfy his needs. In fact, Nick couldn't think of anything that would be less honorable.

"What was it you wanted at this unholy hour, Mother?" he asked with an irritated snap in his voice. He immediately thought better of it and began to apologize for being rude, but his mother didn't give him a chance.

"I'm on my way there, son. I'm concerned about you. The pilot tells me we'll be arriving right after lunch, and I'd appreciate it if you would pick me up at the airstrip."

Nick took a breath. "Mother, there's no need…"

"Nonsense. I want to see you."

"But Annie is living in the pool house. It will be too crowded for you to move in there as well."

"Her quarters still have not been repaired?"

"No, there were other more pressing construction needs." And Nick had been putting off fixing Annie's suite until the very last minute. He wasn't entirely sure he could stand knowing she was sleeping in the same house and not act on his weaknesses.

"Well, never mind that," his mother quipped. "Annie and I will get along famously. It'll be like summer camp with my sisters when I was a girl."

"But…"

His mother bid him a fast goodbye. And Nick was left quietly swearing as the dial tone droned in his ears.

"So how's the construction coming along, *dervla?*" Her mother's voice resonating from the phone's earpiece at once soothed and distressed Annie.

In the six weeks since the hurricane, Annie was growing weary of endless cerulean skies, of baking heat that hovered in the nineties and of stifling humidity that closed in around her and made breathing difficult. She supposed it was partly the humidity and partly her depression that caused her to be so tired all the time.

In self-defense, Annie had made it a point not to see Nick any more often than was absolutely necessary.

When she wasn't working, she stayed by herself in the pool house, reading or answering letters. Except for lately, when she hadn't been able to finish reading even one page without falling sound asleep.

"I didn't wake you did I, honey?" her mother asked when Annie had left her first question unanswered for too long. "What time is it there?"

As if she'd been splashed with cold water, Annie shot upright and looked at the clock—9:00 a.m. She was a half hour late to meet the team in the lagoon.

"We're only an hour ahead of you here, Ma," she said into the portable phone while jumping out of bed and heading for the bathroom. "And I can't talk right now. I'm late for work."

"Are you feeling all right? It's not like you to be late."

"I'm fine. But the heat has been getting to me."

"South Boston has been hot, too. Why don't you just cool off in the ocean?"

Annie wished it was that easy, but the heat and humidity dogged her wherever she went. "I've gotta go, Ma. I'll call you later."

She dashed into the shower and out again in record time. Pulling her hair back in a ponytail and pinning the flyaway strands down, she hurried to step into her swimming suit. But when she dragged it up her hips, she was astounded to discover the darn thing felt too tight.

Could it have shrunk? That didn't seem likely since she'd been wearing it every other day for weeks. If anything, all this wearing and washing should've stretched it out.

Shoving the suit back down her legs, Annie eyed the bathroom scale and decided to give it a try. She might have been eating a tiny bit more than usual lately. But she'd chalked her ravenous hunger up to boredom and the heat.

Until she stepped on the scale. Oh my gosh. She'd gained eight pounds in the past six weeks.

The thought made her slightly queasy, but not enough to stop from grabbing a candy bar and some cheese crackers on her way to the closet to find something else to wear. She hurried into a pair of shorts and a T-shirt that felt a little tight but still fit around her middle.

Jamming her running shoes on her feet and deciding to think about her weight later, Annie headed out the door at a dead run. She nearly knocked both herself and Nick off their feet when they smacked right into each other on the other side of the door.

He reached out and steadied her. "Are you all right?"

"You're the second person to ask me that today," she said as she pulled away from him. "I'm fine. Just late."

Nick studied her face for a moment. "You don't look fine. You look exhausted. Have you been working too hard?"

Her stomach was doing flip-flops at the mere sight of him. And she felt her heart skip as it started beating in double time.

In the morning light, he looked so good she nearly drooled. Tall, handsome and tanned from working outdoors, the sight of the man she cared so much about made her whole body tighten and her mouth start to water.

"Annie?"

Had he asked something? The hunger she'd been feeling became a violent stomach roll all of a sudden.

"Excuse me, Nick." She turned and stepped back inside the door, determined to reach the pool house bathroom in a hurry.

"But I wanted to…"

"Later, please," Annie pleaded.

She slammed the door behind her and made a mad dash to the bathroom, getting there just as the entire contents of her stomach came back up with a powerful whoosh. Well, of all the embarrassing things.

Rinsing her mouth out with water, Annie wondered if she had picked up a bug. But she had no fever. And actually, she felt just fine now that her stomach was empty.

Maybe it had been caused by too much junk food. That might be the correct reason for the weight gain, too.

But when she raised her head and looked in the mirror, she saw a stranger staring back at her. No, wait, stranger wasn't the right word.

Her eyes were a bit sunken in her head, but it *was* her face, just rounder and softer from the added weight. Staring down at the neckline of her square-necked T-shirt, Annie was amazed at how her breasts had suddenly become what could only be called voluptuous.

Weird. None of the girls in her family ever had big breasts until they…

Gasping, Annie beheld the truth in the mirror. She saw her sisters, Kelly and Colleen, grown round and glowing with their pregnancies—and looking right out of the mirror behind her eyes, laughing hysterically at her expense.

In shock, Annie put a hand to her mouth. Then she put the other hand across her belly. Oh my gosh.

Later this afternoon she would get someone from the research team to drive her down to the village store for a pregnancy test kit. But she really didn't need a test to tell her what was clearly written all over her.

She was going to have a baby. And regardless of what he'd told her, she was going to have Nick's baby.

Dear Lord. Now what?

Nick backed away from her door after Annie slammed it in his face. He'd wanted to tell her about his mother's arrival today. But then he'd been blinded by the sight of the faint purple smudges under her eyes, and of her neon pink shirt, and of her face that was somehow glowing and more beautiful than he had ever seen.

He needed to walk away from her now while he could still fight off the furious desire that was buckling his knees. He almost hated her for doing this to him, for being everything that Christina wasn't, and for being the most desirable woman he'd ever known. But he couldn't.

The sad fact was that he was the one to blame for not being able to control his own yearnings. Angry at himself, he jumped into his Jeep and headed down to the latest construction site in the village.

When he'd given Annie the responsibility for the dolphin center, he'd imagined that would be the best answer for both of them. But now he wondered if he had been selfish to want to keep her near enough for him to see, yet hold her far enough away so that there would be no chance of pulling her back into his life.

It couldn't be the best thing for her, staying here on this isolated island and not getting the opportunity to go out in the world to find friends and perhaps a man who would love her forever.

That troubling thought made him slow the Jeep and ball his fists against the steering wheel. The very idea of Annie with another man made him suddenly mad as hell. But he had just better get over it.

Annie had told him that she imagined him as a story-book prince, bewitched and waiting for a princess to come break the spell. Hell. He didn't need to read that damned gypsy's fairy-tale book to know he'd been acting more like a mean old ogre. A beast, like the one in that old tale of the beauty and the beast, who locked up beautiful women and never let them leave the castle.

Blowing out a breath, he decided to give the whole thing some more thought. But not until after his mother had left the island again. It was too hard to think with her nearby. Almost as difficult as being around Annie.

Almost, but not exactly the same.

"The island doesn't look too terribly shabby," his mother said as he pulled in to the lot beside the pool house. "The trees will take some time to grow back, but all in all it's much better than I'd imagined. You must've worked round the clock to get the work done."

He shook his head. "I've had lots of help. The island-ers have been amazing."

His mother smiled. "My great-great-grandfather always thought so, too. He said there were no better people anywhere on earth than the families he'd hired to come work and live here."

Nick forgot from time to time that it was his mother's family who had owned this island for generations. His father had always been such a huge presence in his life that he was shocked to remember that it was his mother who had inherited all the money from her wealthy American ancestors.

"Well, here we are," he told her as he parked the Jeep and got out to carry her luggage. "I doubt Annie will be here to greet you. In the afternoons she can usually be found down at the lagoon, working with the dolphins."

His mother shot him a very strange look before she shrugged her shoulder and climbed out of the Jeep. "That's fine, dear. It will give me a chance to settle in. I'll look forward to dining with her later."

"Well..." Nick filled his arms with his mother's luggage and followed her as she unlocked the door and stepped inside. "I don't know if..."

Just as his eyes adjusted to the cool interior of the three-room pool house, Annie came flying out of the bathroom and nearly knocked into his mother.

Her eyes filled with confusion for a second, then she grinned and hugged his mother. "Oh, Mrs. Scoville. I'm so glad to see you."

His mother gave Annie a kiss on the cheek and held her at arm's length to study her. "It's wonderful to see you again, my dear. I've been quite eager for us to have a nice chat. Would you care to join me for a cup of tea?"

"Uh, can it be later, please? I have to go back to work now." Annie pulled out of his mother's grasp, nodded to him and ran out the door.

He dropped his mother's bags and dashed outside after Annie. "Wait a second," he muttered as he caught her by the arm. "What's so urgent that you can't spend a few moments to talk to my mother?"

She tugged against his grip then spun around when he refused to release her arm. "Nick, please. I have to go now. I'm sorry."

Studying her eyes, he saw they were overly bright and the remnants of tears lay caught in her lashes. "At least tell me what's wrong. Maybe there's something I can do."

"You've already done it," she said on a deep breath.

He stared down at her, wanting desperately to wrap her up in his arms and make whatever troubled her go away. "What have I done? Just stand still a second and talk to me. Are you sick?"

She laughed, but the sound was more like a strangled sob. "For the third time today, I'm fine, dammit." Yanking her arm out of his grip, she flipped her loose hair back off her shoulder. "I'm not sick—just pregnant."

It took a second for her words to sink into his thick skull. "What? You can't be."

Laughing again, she swiped a hand over her face and cleared away a lone tear. "Just had the test. It's official. I guess your doctors didn't know what they were talking about when they said you couldn't have a child."

He stood there, dumbfounded, for much too long. Long enough to see the rejection and hurt fill her eyes.

"Sorry to spring it on you, Nick, but you insisted. And I really have to go now." She turned and rushed away toward the lagoon.

Leaving him stunned—and more than a little baffled. Damn it all to hell.

Seven

Nick's feet were glued to the patio, his brain frozen and unable to function. Was it possible Annie was going to have a child? And more to the point, that he was going to be a father?

"Is that a real possibility, son?" The soft voice came from behind his back, echoing his thoughts.

Uh-oh. He didn't want to turn around and have to face his mother, who had obviously overheard Annie's announcement. What would he say?

What *could* he say? Something like: *So sorry. I took advantage of an employee. And at the time, she was a nice young, naive virgin. Isn't that just the kind of honorable thing you always wanted for your only son?*

Letting out a breath, Nick turned around to face his mother and to begin facing the consequences of his actions.

"Do you mean, is it possible that Annie is pregnant?" he asked, hedging for time. "I cannot imagine that she would lie about such a thing, Mother."

His mother's violet eyes were filled with questions. But beyond those, she had a kind of bewildered but blissful expression on her face. It made him feel ashamed all of a sudden.

"But if you meant, is it possible that the child is mine," he rushed out with a huff. "I don't know. The doctors in Alsaca were quite positive that my sperm count ranged too low to be effective. But…"

He had to clear his head and begin accepting facts, but how could he when his mother kept looking at him that way? "On the other hand, I have no doubts that any baby Annie would be having from her time on the is-land must be…my child." There. He'd said it.

His stomach rolled and he was beginning to feel dizzy. He had too many unanswered questions of his own to talk about this just yet, especially with his mother.

"Come back inside with me for a few minutes, Nicholas," his mother said as she gently touched his arm. "You look like you need to sit down."

Blinded by shock, Nick let her guide him inside the pool house. The front room was laid out like a small apartment with a kitchen and seating area.

All the thoughts in his head at the moment were of babies. Little boys with fiery red curls, running outside to play with Annie's exuberance. And little girls, with her deep green eyes, lifting their arms to him for a hug.

After they were seated at the tiny two person table,

his mother took his hand. "You never said anything before about what the Alsaca doctors told you.

I suspected there was a problem with Christina being able to conceive, but now everything makes more sense."

"What makes sense?" To Nick, the whole world was upside down. Nothing made any sense at all.

"Your isolation from the world. Your determination to open this marine mammal center."

"I was just trying to honor Christina's wishes…her memory." A small flame of anger lit in his gut at his mother's pop-psychology attempts.

"No, Nicholas. It's all been built on your guilt about not being able to have a child. I'll wager it has something to do with disappointing your father."

He stood and fisted his hands in his pockets. "I really don't want to talk about this right now."

"Oh, but you should. Talking is the best way to think through a situation."

"No, Mother. Stop trying to meddle."

She looked up at him with disappointment in her eyes. "Just let me say a few things then. First, I want you to go down to the village clinic and discuss your physical situation with Dr. Gamble. Let him help you understand."

When Nick started to argue, she broke in again. "I realize he's just a small-town family physician, but you've known him all your life. And I know you trust his knowledge and expertise the same way I do. Do it for me."

He hung his head. "Yes, all right. I can do that."

"Good. And afterward, I insist you go and discuss

this situation with Annie. She's a fine young woman who didn't deserve your terrible silence when she told you nothing but the truth. I have no idea what has transpired between you…" she hesitated and then stood up and touched his hand.

"Well, I can imagine some of it. But regardless of whatever else you are, son, you are an honorable man. I expect you to ask Annie what she wants to do and then to move heaven and earth in order to abide by her wishes."

"Do?" As in the future? He hadn't thought that far ahead. And couldn't imagine doing it now, either.

"Think over the possibilities on your way to see the doctor. You may want to ask him any questions you have about that, too."

"All right. Fine. Anything else?" His irritation was growing and he needed some air.

His mother stretched up on tiptoes to give him a kiss. "I love you, Nicholas. You and Annie have created my first grandchild."

The guilt came back with a force that nearly knocked him to his knees. "I would appreciate it if you did not mention this to Father," he said though gritted teeth. "In fact, don't discuss it with anyone until I can speak to Annie."

His mother studied him for a second. "I agree, son. You must be the one to tell your father about this. But would it anger you if I talked to Annie about the subject before you do?"

"No meddling, Mother."

When she looked wounded, he relented and gave her a hug. "Yes, perhaps you can give her some advice, or at least give her an opportunity to talk it over with another woman. But you are not to pressure her in any way. Is that clear?"

"Perfectly, Nicholas." She kissed him again. "Now go ask your questions of the doctor and think about what you want to do. I believe you're going to make a wonderful father."

A father? He hadn't yet even considered the ramifications of that. He'd thought about Annie being a good mother, but him a father?

Now that the biology of fathering a child appeared to have happened, Nick had to wonder what kind of father he would really make. His own father's example was not one Nick wanted to follow. The man was a control freak, a tyrant.

Nick's whole life had been spent trying to please his father. To no avail. Never good enough. Never smart enough. The only thing that he'd ever done right in his father's opinion was to marry Christina.

And now? Now he was about to become a father without even the benefit of marriage. He could just imagine what his father would have to say about that.

Hell.

Annie made it all the way through the afternoon's work at the lagoon without breaking down. But now she found herself standing alone at the ocean's edge right before dusk on the verge of panic.

She loved being here on the island, with its hazy blue skies and brilliant aquamarine waters. But she had to give some consideration to where she would go and what she would do now that she was expecting a baby.

The thought of going home to her family snuck in and then back out of her mind. They were going to be terribly disappointed with her predicament. She just couldn't bear thinking of the hurt looks in their eyes when she told them the truth. As much as she loved them all deeply, South Boston was the last place she would go now.

She'd escaped the tenterhooks of home once. And that was tough enough, what with everyone convinced that she would never make it on her own.

But Annie knew she'd grown strong and independent since she'd moved a million light years away from her childhood. And she was sure she would be able to figure out some other way rather than running back to her family.

She thought about the large savings account she'd built up from her wages here, and absently placed a protective hand against her stomach. There would be two of them to consider from now on.

So how would having a baby affect her career? Annie imagined that being a personal trainer would be pretty much out of the question for a while. What else could she do to support herself and a child?

A big part of her was thrilled and excited at the prospect of becoming a mother. It was something that every little girl dreamed about, including her. She loved her nieces and nephews and babysat for them all the time back in South Boston. Holding a baby in her arms brought wonderful maternal urges that had always made Annie secretly covet her sister's lives.

Yes, that part was thrilling all right. But another part of her was afraid. Afraid of seeing societies' reaction to her single motherhood. Her life was definitely not going down the road of any fairy-tale now.

And what would Nick's reaction be when he overcame his initial shock? Would he want to participate in his child's life? Or would he want to be rid of them both so he would not have to be reminded of his indiscretions?

With thoughts reeling and emotions raging, Annie turned around to head back up the cliff toward the house. She saw Nick's mother standing on the patio, watching her.

Darn it. Mrs. Scoville must've heard her talking to Nick. Facing the embarrassment of Nick's mother knowing of their…uh…affair before she had a chance to sort out her own feelings was the last thing Annie wanted to do.

But Mrs. Scoville had always been most gracious and kind. And Annie knew she had nowhere to run anyway.

With the red blush crawling up her neck and about to strangle her, Annie slowly climbed the few steps to the patio. All she could do was pray that the normally nice, civilized woman would not be angry about the fact that Annie had seduced her only son.

"You looked so distraught and lonely out on the beach all by yourself," Mrs. Scoville said as she reached out for her. "Please come have tea with me. Talk to me. Let me help you." She placed her arm around Annie's waist and propped her up as they walked back toward the pool house.

Annie leaned against the older woman's warmth and sighed. This is what she might've wished her mother would do for her. Comfort her. Baby her.

But Maeve Mary Margaret O'Brien Riley would no doubt grab her up by the hair and throw her into a convent instead. No, this kind of comfort and intimacy would never come at the hands of her own mother. And the other members of her family wouldn't dare go against the matriarch.

There would be no long talks on the phone to her sisters. No emergency consultations with her grandmother on what to do for morning sickness. Annie vowed not to mention it to them at all until after the baby was born.

She let Nick's mother lead her into the pool house, where a silver tea cart sat laden with small sandwiches and steaming milk. It was such a welcoming sight that Annie nearly broke down and cried.

"Sit here, dear," Mrs. Scoville said. "Or would you be more comfortable having a shower before you take tea?"

There was such an obvious look of concern in the other woman's eyes that Annie immediately released the tension she'd been holding. It was the best she could've hoped for, and she suddenly felt much safer than she had only a few minutes before.

"I missed lunch today and lost everything I'd had in my stomach before that. I'm starved. Could we just eat first?"

"Certainly. Please sit down. I'll pour." Mrs. Scoville fussed over her and made sure she had what she needed before she joined her at the table.

Annie wolfed down a couple of finger sandwiches and followed them with a cup of warm milk garnished with a dash of tea and sugar. Already she was beginning to feel more human.

"I have to apologize for my son's actions this afternoon," Mrs. Scoville began when Annie leaned back in her chair. "In his defense, I can only say that this must have been as big a shock to you as it was for him. But he will step up and stand beside you in the end. At his core, he is driven to be noble."

"Oh I know that," Annie said with surprise. She'd never had any real doubts about him doing whatever he saw as his duty. It had just been the first rush of panic that made her go crazy with doubt.

The older woman smiled, but then her expression turned wary. "Have you…" Mrs. Scoville hesitated, looking conflicted and concerned. "Well, have you considered all your first options?"

"Options?" What was she asking? "If you mean about where I want to live after the baby is born, no. I thought I'd wait and see what Nick wants us to do. I'll try to abide by his wishes. If he wants us to live close enough that he can visit his child, we'll…"

"You intend to have this child then," Mrs. Scoville interrupted. She released a deep breath and smiled.

"What? Of course. You didn't think…" Annie nearly came up off her chair before she calmed down and realized the woman didn't really know her all that well. "That was never an *option*. I not only intend to have this child, I intend to raise it, with or without anyone's help."

The older woman placed a hand over hers and smiled again. "The rest of your decisions should be made together with Nicholas. But I can assure you that neither you nor my grandchild will ever want for anything."

Her grandchild? Oh my gosh. Suddenly, this baby was becoming very real. That spurt of panic was back.

She was actually going to be a mother. And perhaps a single mom, at that.

"I didn't have any daughters," Mrs. Scoville continued in a soothing voice. "But I did have a baby once, and I have a sister who had a child. Will you allow me the privilege of assisting you with this pregnancy? We may have to learn some of the newer methods and ideas together…"

She stopped speaking and tilted her head to study Annie. "Perhaps you would prefer to go home to your own mother to await your child?"

"No." Annie answered with way too much force. "No," she said again, softer this time and with a smile. "I'd be really grateful if you'd let me stay here on the island until the baby is born, Mrs. Scoville. And believe me, I'll gladly take whatever advice you want to give."

Mrs. Scoville's eyes filled with tears, but she chuckled and patted Annie's hand. "Wonderful. I just know you and Nicholas will be able to work something out."

She stood and pulled the softly colored afghan off the back of the sofa and placed it on Annie's lap. "Now, let's begin by you calling me Elizabeth. This is going to be such fun. I can hardly wait."

Eight

The next morning at sunrise Nick made his way to the pool house to talk to Annie. His visit to Dr. Gamble yesterday afternoon had been eye-opening. But he was still in shock and hadn't slept, trying desperately to focus on what would be the best thing for everyone.

He had no way of knowing yet what Annie would want to do. But Nick could only hope she wouldn't want to go back to her family in Boston on a permanent basis. When the doctor had confirmed that it was entirely possible for a man with a low sperm count to conceive a child with a fertile woman, Nick had been more confused than ever about what the right move would be.

Trying to imagine what it would be like to be a father, he wanted to see into the future. To envision what a child of his and Annie's making would be like.

But instead of thinking of children, he thought of Annie, with her zest for life and her colorful nature. It made him remember her, lying naked beside him with fire in her eyes. She'd had eyes for only him then, and wanted him.

An old familiar wedge of guilt drove straight into his soul. Thinking about Annie only caused a lustful hunger to bubble up deep in his gut. Again.

He couldn't believe he'd let things with her get so out of hand during the storm. He'd betrayed Christina's memory, dishonored Annie and had probably disappointed his parents beyond redemption.

However, all this introspection was useless. There was nothing to do now but swallow the regret and discuss the problem with Annie.

Before he raised his hand to knock on the pool house door, he peeked through a window into the front room to see if anyone was awake yet. Annie normally would be up at this hour, but in her condition would she rather sleep late?

He saw her, with that graceful athlete's back to him, dressed in shorts and standing in front of the small kitchenette with hands firmly fisted on her hips. She'd tied her fiery curls back with a band, but several wispy strands still escaped down her neck to give her a feminine and fairy-tale princess look.

Gulping back the immediate lash of hot desire that went straight to his groin, Nick forced his gaze away and softly knocked on the door. Their discussion had to remain all business. His lust for her had already landed them in a huge predicament. One he had no idea how to fix.

Annie opened the door and gazed up at him. He felt his body sway toward those deep luminous green pools and had to reach out to steady himself by holding the edge of the door.

"We need to discuss things," he heard his own voice saying from far away.

"Outside, please," she whispered. "I don't want to wake your mother. We were up late talking and I know she must be jet-lagged."

He stood aside and let her slip out of the door before he closed it behind her. It took every bit of his control not to touch her as she passed by and started out ahead of him toward the cliff stairs.

Annie sat down on the top stair and stared out at the first rays of orange dawn peeking out over the ocean. She turned back when he came up behind her and motioned for him to sit beside her.

He would rather stand, thank you. Getting too close to her had not proven to be the safest thing for him to do in the past.

Nick went down three steps and turned around to talk, almost face-to-face at this level. It was too close to suit him, but at least he wouldn't have to touch her.

"I thought I had better start out by apologizing for my actions during the storm, Annie." He fisted his hands and stuck them in his pockets. "This is all my—"

"Stop it, Nick," she warned. "My being pregnant is every bit as much my own fault as it is yours. I didn't have to say yes. And as a matter of fact, as I recall, it was me that begged you and not the other way around."

He blinked twice and simply stared at her. Somehow his voice had been lost in the middle of her little speech.

"I know you're feeling guilty here," she rushed on. "But don't. It makes me wonder if I shouldn't be feeling guilty myself, and I refuse to do that. And I don't need your pity either, thanks. I don't want you to put yourself out on my account.

"I'm a grown woman who can take care of herself," she continued. "Your mother has invited me to stay on the island until the baby is born, which I intend to do unless you have major objections. After that, I'm not sure what I'll do, but I would never keep you away from your child if you wanted to see it from time to time." She hesitated and looked up at him with huge, wary eyes.

"Annie," he said softly. Her vulnerability and the nervous habit she had of talking too fast made his heart ache. Everything was clear to him all of sudden. There was only one thing that would ever make this situation right.

"I would never be able to rest not knowing how you two were getting along every day," he told her with a quiet plea in his voice. "Let me be with you, take care of both of you—and do what's right. Marry me."

"What?" Her eyes blazed at him and she stood up. "I just told you I could take care of myself. You don't need to be some kind of martyr and marry a woman you don't love. We will be fine."

He'd had a feeling she was going to say that. One little part of him breathed a big sigh of relief. But another large part of him refused to pay attention.

Nick climbed the stair to be on her level and took her lightly by the shoulders. "As you no doubt recall, I don't believe that love is a necessary requirement for getting married. But honor and fidelity are the best reasons I know of for two people to make a commitment to each other.

"Let me honor you, and honor our child," he continued.

She looked as if he'd struck her rather than tried to do the right thing. So vulnerable and alone it almost brought tears to his eyes, she bowed her head and sighed.

He rushed ahead, knowing he could push her over the edge now. "Return the favor and do me the honor of becoming my wife, Annie Riley."

He held his breath for a moment, almost convincing himself it would be better if she turned him down.

Annie lifted her chin and looked at him. "Yes."

"What?" There was a whooshing sound in his ears and he wasn't sure he'd heard her right. He dropped his hands.

She laughed, but it sounded hollow. "My answer is yes. I will marry you, Nick. Sure you don't wanna take it back?"

"No," he answered with a raspy voice. He cleared his throat a couple of times before he tried again. "No, of course not. I want to be sure you two are okay. I…"

"And I'm just old-fashioned enough to want my child to have a father," Annie interrupted. "So when do you want to do it?"

"Do it?"

"Get married."

His head was thumping and his blood was running hot and cold, but he shook it off and tried to focus. "As soon as possible, I guess. Uh…where would you like to have the ceremony take place? Here? Boston?"

"Here. I…I'm ashamed for my mother to find out and I don't want to tell anyone in my family until after we're married. It'll be easier on everyone that way."

The whole thing was beginning to sound dirty and way too dry for such a sacred ceremony. But then again, it was him that had wanted them to stay on a business-like level.

He reached for her but she turned her back. "Go away for now, Nick. We can work out the details later."

Did she want him to hold her? Perhaps seal the deal with a kiss the way it was in her books? He was afraid to touch her. Afraid he might actually break down if she cried in his arms.

"I'll call the village magistrate and work it out," he said to her back. "It will be okay, Annie. I promise."

And God help him, he would move heaven and earth as he'd promised his mother to make it so. For Annie.

Annie held herself together until she heard Nick's footsteps walking away. Running down the stairs to the isolated beach, she finally let her tears flow.

Not sure what she'd expected when Nick turned up at her door at sunrise, a proposal of marriage hadn't even been on the list of possibilities. In the back of her mind, she supposed what she'd imagined was that he would offer money to support his child—support both of them—as long as they were somewhere on the other side of the world.

When he'd popped the question, though, marriage suddenly seemed the right thing to do. They shared romantic ideals of family and both of them had prehistoric notions that children needed two parents.

When they'd talked during the hurricane about his first wife wanting a baby, the look on his face had been clear enough. He'd wanted a child, too.

But did he want a new wife? Did he really want her?

Standing at the water's edge, she looked out as the sky completed the change from the periwinkle-blue of pre-dawn to the rose and gold glow of morning. But the beauty she beheld only made the ache in her heart grow stronger.

Tears streamed down her cheeks, as she wondered why things had to be so complicated. Why couldn't she and Nick have fallen in love, then gotten married and had sex, and then had a baby? That was the way it was in fairy tales.

She sniffed and wound her arms around her middle. Grow up, Annie girl. Life is not a fairy tale. No one had ever even hinted that it would be.

She'd said yes to his proposal to quell her panic at being a single mother. Marrying Nick would save her reputation and give her back her family. And maybe their marriage would work out okay in the end.

So what if he could be the most annoying man in the world at times. She respected Nick more than she could say. And she trusted him to take care of her and their baby—even though he'd made it clear he didn't love or need her.

He was honorable and reliable and rich.

Instead of those thoughts calming her tears, a sob ripped from her throat and the watery flow increased. Oh, God, how she wished he would love her like her father loved her mother. That's what she'd always dreamed about. A Prince Charming whose love would grow stronger each day.

But it was not to be for her. No. She was preparing

to marry a man who didn't love her at all. Wouldn't let himself love her, even though she was half in love with him already.

A nasty image of the future jumped into her mind. Since Nick didn't love her, would it be possible that the ghost of his first wife and her unfulfilled desires could come back to haunt him someday? When Annie's baby came, would it just serve to remind him of how much he wished it was Christina having his child?

Annie didn't think she could accept being married to a man who couldn't bear the sight of her and only stayed married for the child's sake.

Nick would always honor his duty to their child, Annie knew that. But her family was not going to be of any use to Nick's father. Their marriage would not be a meeting of business entities. Without love, they would have nothing to hold them together the way he'd had when he first married Christina.

Annie sniffed back what she hoped were the last of her tears. She'd gotten herself into this mess. If she and Nick became strangers after the baby came, she would just have to get herself back out of it again.

It would absolutely kill her to have to live with him and love him, knowing full well that he couldn't stand being with her.

Love him? Damn it. So it *was* love that she had already been feeling toward him.

Love. How scary was that?

The tears began again in earnest. Oh heaven help her.

What a mess. Divorce was almost as terrifying a phrase in her family as unwed mother. But what else could she do if it came to that?

Sighing, she knew her hormones were raging and making her a complete mess at the moment. But she simply had to think this through before she made a move.

Her child needed a name and a father. And she really wanted a chance to build a life with Nick. Maybe she could find a way to make him want to keep her in his life, too. Perhaps she could weave a little Irish magic around him and make him need her. Maybe...

Okay, she could do this. She would take the chance on Nick. And just pray she would be strong enough to find a way out if things got unbearable.

Later that afternoon after work, Annie found herself at the village clinic getting a premarital checkup. Nick had disappeared after his own exam, saying he would be back to pick her up in a while.

"You're a fine healthy young woman, Annie," Doctor Gamble told her. "You should have no trouble carrying this child and as many more as you and Nick decide to have."

The idea of having more children depressed her. She'd always wanted to have at least four. But those thoughts would have to wait until she saw what happened in her marriage after the first one arrived on the scene.

"Should I expect to limit my physical activities in the later stages of the pregnancy? I want to keep working with the dolphins and I just love being in the ocean. Will I have to stop at some point?"

"I really don't see any reason why you couldn't keep going as long as you feel well. The last couple of weeks before your due date you might want to slow down some, but swimming is good for you as long as you don't overdo it.

"I'm not sure how Nick is going to handle your spending so much time in the water, though," the doctor continued.

She stopped rebuttoning her blouse and looked at the doctor. "You mean because his first wife drowned? I know he hasn't been able to get back in the water himself, but that shouldn't have anything to do with me. I'm a terrific swimmer."

"So was Christina. So was Nick, for that matter. In fact, he was a world-class yachtsman up until the accident. Christina's avocation was marine science research. Nick's was captaining an America's Cup contender."

"Really? He's never mentioned sailing."

"He wouldn't. Nick was the one that insisted Christina learn to crew for his team. She didn't like all that speed and the need for such quick response times."

The doctor hesitated a moment and studied Annie. "Nick blames himself for her death. He's given up yachting."

Oh dear. Now that really was just too sad to contemplate. Besides losing his wife, he also felt guilty enough about her drowning to give up his love of sailing. Annie felt the melancholy creeping over her once more. Poor, cheerless lost soul.

A lump formed in her chest and worked its way up into her throat. She'd been selfish, worrying about marrying a man who didn't love her. He was noble and hurt and, well, she would have to stop thinking of her own problems and start trying to make his life better.

"Maybe I can help him get over his fear of water," she told the doctor. That was only one small thing she intended to do to help him.

Doctor Gamble tilted his head and smiled. "You know, I think maybe you might just be the one to do that."

Nick was driving his Jeep on their way back to the main house. "You're awfully quiet," he said to her after ten long minutes of utter silence. "Are you unhappy about the wedding plans?"

The sky was overcast, and whenever the ocean came into view, tiny whitecaps frothed the water as if it were the top of a newly poured glass of beer. Annie had been daydreaming about finding a way to break the evil spell Nick was under.

Maybe that's why she'd found her way to this island in the first place. She could've been sent here by some magic in order to bring him back into the world.

Nick took her hand. "Are you okay with getting married by the magistrate the day after tomorrow? Would you rather fly to the States and find a priest to marry us?"

"What? No. Thanks for asking, Nick, but a priest would want us to go through classes and preparations. Being married the day after tomorrow will be better."

He pulled the Jeep in beside the pool house and turned to face her. "Annie, I'm sorry this wedding won't be like the ones you've always dreamed about. But I want to make it as special as I can on such short notice. Will you let me try?"

Lifting her hand to his mouth, he turned it over and

tenderly kissed her palm. As he did, he lifted his eyes—those twinkling, smiling blues—to check her reaction.

And boy was she reacting. Tiny tingles shot all over her body, just as if she'd been dropped whole into the same frothy beer glass that was foaming up the ocean.

In the next moment, Nick's look turned sweet instead of hot. "You and my mother can take care of your wedding outfit. I'll do everything else." He released her hand and grinned. "Just plan on meeting me back at the magistrate's office at 10:00 a.m. the day after tomorrow, okay?"

She nodded, struck dumb by his beautiful, sincere expression.

"Good." He turned to open the door, but thought of something else and turned back to her. "You will be moving back into the main house after the wedding. Back to my bed. Won't you?"

"If that's what you want, Nick." Even though she said those words and had agreed, the nagging thought that they were rushing into something began to swim in her head.

He stilled and frowned at her. "I want you to want it as well. I intend for our marriage to be a real one."

"Do you?" She had never wanted anything more in her life. But she had a queasy feeling that it wouldn't be that simple. "Then I'll be glad to move back to your bed."

If there was one good thing they had together, it was sex.

As far as the rest of their lives went…well…they would just have to see how strong this spell was compared to how badly she wanted to break it.

The next two days went by in a blur for Nick. He couldn't remember when he'd had such fun. Planning a quickie wedding didn't take much effort. But planning for a reception and honeymoon that was designed especially for Annie took a lot of thought and then some fast action.

His mother had helped with a few of the ideas, but he'd molded them to fit Annie's personality. He'd contacted people he hadn't even thought of in years. People who seemed genuinely pleased to help.

And he found ways to spend more money in two days than he'd spent in the past two years. Grinning to himself, he'd decided it had been a pure pleasure. It made him wonder why he hadn't thought to have this kind of fun before now?

The answer hit him dead center between the eyes, and dropped like a anchor straight to his heart. Christina.

She had never cared about money or the things it could buy. Their marriage ceremony had certainly been a huge, overinflated and expensive production. But it hadn't been planned by either one of them. Their parents had made all the arrangements.

During the years they were married, Christina never cared about material things and had even seemed rather bored when receiving gifts. At the time, Nick thought he admired her for rejecting her parents' devotion to money and the things it could buy.

But looking back, he remembered that never being able to give her anything had created a terrible frustration inside of him. There was nothing he could ever have done to make her happy.

In fact, the only time he remembered seeing Christina smile was when he agreed that she could come here to the island to live and build her research center. It had finally been something he could truly give her.

But she'd meant to live here permanently—without him. When at last he'd figured out her real intention, he came to the island to confront her and demand she find something else that she would enjoy doing—with him.

A cold sweat of guilt suddenly broke over Nick, leaving him blinded by the demons of memories. Everything he'd ever found pleasure in had been tainted by his selfishness toward Christina.

Sailing. The ocean. His work in Alsaca.

Now, instead of honoring her memory the way he'd intended, soberly and quietly, he was actually enjoying himself and spending money in a way that Christina would not have approved. He gulped down the ache that lodged itself in his chest and squared his shoulders.

His child was on the way, he reminded himself sternly. And a woman, who was very much alive, needed him to be strong. In a few short hours he and Annie would be married.

Though they would be marrying without love, Nick was determined that their relationship would not only be filled with honor, the same way his parents' marriage was, but would also be built around respect and trust. Whenever he looked into Annie's eyes, he was sure that he could trust her.

If he could just manage to control his own selfish desires, Annie would never have to suggest that they separate to find happiness. Their relationship would last.

He would just have to put all the black memories of his failure with Christina into a corner of his mind.

Then he could pull them out to inspect in some future quiet moment when it was much more appropriate. And remind himself of the error of his ways.

Nine

Annie's knees were shaking as she stood with Nick's mother in the anteroom of the three-room single-story building that served as the island's courthouse, magistrate's office and jail. It was going to take more than a magic spell to get her through this ceremony in one piece.

Where were all the leprechauns and elves with their magic when you needed them the most?

She still had a few minutes left to back out of the deal. But for the past hour, Elizabeth had not been far from her side, and had been keeping a firm hand on her shoulder. Annie couldn't bear to see the older woman be disappointed.

Nick's mother had been so kind, helping her choose this princess-style dress from a store in St. Thomas. It wasn't all that fancy, made out of a sheer cotton and not cut from silk or satin. But it was long, down to her ankles, and was the most gorgeous swirling shades of amethyst and evergreen Annie had ever seen.

She felt like a real story-book heroine in this dress. And not at all like a woman who was about to be sentenced to live a long, dreary life without love.

Running away was out of the question. Annie had to keep reminding herself that she was still on an island with nowhere to run.

Just then, she heard a flute begin to play. The music was an otherworldly sound and gave her chills. But within minutes the melancholy sounds were joined by other instruments and the beat turned noisily happy instead of quietly sad.

The music itself seemed so out place in this tiny austere office space that Annie nearly giggled as the pace picked up. A grin spread out over her face and she wondered for a second if she was dreaming.

"That's an Irish jig," she exclaimed, turning to Elizabeth for confirmation.

"Yes, he's trying hard to please you," Nick's mother replied with a bittersweet smile. "You may have to give him a little time to come around, sweetheart. His guilt is still fresh and stays quite near the surface. It drives him to be a bit too pushy. But he does care for you."

Time, Annie thought with chagrin. She'd never been known for her patience.

But the idea that he had gone out of his way to find a musician to play special tunes just for her, managed to calm her nerves. The panic was stashed aside for the time being.

"I care for him too, Elizabeth," she said quietly. "As

a matter of fact, I love Nick very much and probably fell for him from the first moment I met him. He can have all the time he needs. The rest of my life if necessary."

The words had come spilling out, but she realized she'd meant them from the bottom of her heart. Annie had been trying to pretend that his not loving her didn't matter. That because she was getting married away from her family in a quickie ceremony, a quickie divorce would be a logical way out if necessary. But now she knew it wasn't true.

It all mattered. Because Nick mattered. Too much.

Nick's mother hugged her tightly. "Thank heaven," she whispered in her ear. "He deserves to be loved like that. But he won't make it easy to love him. His first tendency always is to control the situation and people around him. Just like his father."

Annie leaned back and smiled at her. "Don't worry. That won't change the way I feel."

"Then take a little motherly advice, dear." Elizabeth's eyes were filling with tears but they were also twinkling with happiness. "Don't let him know he has your love just yet. Make him work for it. Drag him kicking and screaming into the freedom of love, chasing you."

The music's tempo changed and the door to the larger courtroom opened. Nick stood there, holding his hand out to her.

"Are you ready?" he asked solemnly. He looked so handsome in his white tuxedo jacket that she nearly broke down and wept.

They hadn't seen each other in two days, but at the

moment it felt more like a lifetime. He had just stepped out of her dreams, looking exactly like the Prince Charming she'd always wished would come sweep her off her feet.

Annie quickly turned and kissed his mother's cheek. "Thank you, Elizabeth. Thank you for everything."

Then she took Nick's hand. "Yes, I'm ready."

Nick managed to get through his vows and held his breath waiting until Annie said hers. He'd asked the magistrate to make the ceremony a little more formal than usual, hoping to please Annie and make it seem more real for her.

He could feel the sweat beading on his forehead and hoped she wouldn't notice his shaky hands when he put the ring on her finger. Everything had to be just right. Nick knew this wasn't the best way to begin a marriage, but he'd be damned if some little detail would go wrong and make her regret that she'd agreed to become his wife.

"Nick?"

Looking down at Annie's sweet face, he tried to focus on what was going on around them. "Huh?"

"The ring, son," the magistrate said with a smile.

"Oh, right." This one was easy.

He'd made a quick trip to the family jeweler in Miami yesterday, but couldn't manage to find anything that looked even remotely like it would belong on Annie's finger. In desperation, he'd gone to his mother for advice. She came up with the perfect solution.

Reaching into his pocket while keeping watch on Annie's expression, he withdrew his great-aunt Lucille's three-carat emerald ring and placed it on her finger. Later he would tell Annie that the moment he'd seen it again he had been positive it should be hers.

As a boy, he'd always found peace whenever he and his mother went to visit Lucille. She was kind and generous and he could hide away from his father's strict rules while he was in her house.

He remembered admiring her ring one day and was amazed when his mother told him Lucille had left it to him to give to his wife. The colors in the gem matched exactly the colors in Annie's eyes.

Annie gasped as she got a good look at the ring on her finger. And when she lifted her eyes to his, he saw something that made him feel much better about this whole wedding.

Annie was happy—truly happy about marrying him. It was as clear as the bright sunshine there in her eyes and it gave him a faint ray of hope that everything would eventually turn out okay. That they could make a life and a home without love.

After a few more words were said, it was time to kiss the bride. This was the part he'd been looking forward to for days—weeks—now.

He reached out and slowly drew her to him. She was as soft as a cloud in his arms. Her breast pressed against his chest and his whole body tightened. Inappropriately.

After giving her a quick, hot kiss, he stepped back. This was not the time or place. Not with his mother, the magistrate and the entire research team in attendance. But Annie blinked her eyes and swayed toward him.

Afraid that she might collapse right here, he took her elbow, pulling her close. "You all right?" he whispered.

"What? Oh, yes. Just a little dizzy." She smiled at him and his own knees wobbled.

"She hasn't eaten much today," his mother said from behind him.

Nick turned to the magistrate. "We're married, right?"

"Yes, sir."

He returned his attention to Annie. "Then your carriage awaits, madame." Waving his arm with a wide flourish he led her out into the bright daylight.

"Oh, Nick, what have you done?" Annie said with a sigh when she saw his Jeep waiting at the door.

Sweeping her up in his arms, he lifted her into the back passenger seat of the completely made-over vehicle. A couple of the island's carpenters had spent the last two days building an old-fashioned carriage over the frame of his old Jeep. There weren't any horses on the island. But other than that small difference, the thing would've passed for something right out of one of her fairy-tale books.

Rob Bellamy drove them through the streets of the village on the way up to the main house. Nick hadn't planned it, but many of the islanders came out to stand by the side of the road and wave as they went by. It seemed to make Annie happy to wave back.

"I feel just like Cinderella," she laughed.

He reached over and took her hand. "You are much more beautiful than any princess in a book."

Her smile faded and she eased her hand from his grasp. "Why didn't your father come to the wedding, Nick? Wasn't there enough time for him to get here? We could've waited an extra day or two for him."

"I didn't invite him," he told her in a voice that sounded rougher than he'd meant. "And since you didn't invite your family, either, I think we're even."

She turned her head and silently stared out the window.

"It'll be just a few more minutes without food," he said, trying to coax her out of her silence. "I don't want you fainting in the middle of your wedding reception."

"We're having a reception?"

"Well, it won't be a huge party. But the chef has been secretly cooking up some pretty exotic dishes for the buffet. I think he wants to impress you."

Annie smiled, but it didn't go all the way to her eyes. "I'm already impressed by him. He's terrifically talented. You're lucky to have him."

And he was beyond lucky to have her as well, he thought. But he didn't know how to tell her that.

"A reception will be wonderful, and it's almost as much a surprise as this carriage was," she told him. "But you didn't need to go to so much trouble. This was just supposed to be a fast, shotgun wedding."

"A shotgun wedding? What's that?"

She laughed and the sound stirred his blood again. "That's an old American saying for a wedding where the bride is already pregnant. It's a kind of joke about her father holding a gun to the groom's head to be sure he doesn't run out on the bride before they can make it legal."

Instead of making him laugh, the idea sobered him. "I don't see that as humorous," he told her. "There should be nothing funny about doing your duty."

"Oh for heaven's sake," she said with a chuckle.

"Lighten up. We're married. You've done your duty and your honor is intact."

He didn't want her first thought to be about responsibility when she remembered this wedding, and he was sorry the subject had come up.

Trying to change it, he said, "I'm glad you liked the carriage idea and the reception should be pleasant enough."

He really hoped the party would be quick, moving them on their way to a surprise honeymoon trip. He couldn't wait to get his hands on Annie once again. To sink into her warmth and slide into her open arms.

"But wait until you find out about your next surprise," he continued with a smile. "That'll be the best one yet."

"Another surprise? It couldn't be as nice as this ring was. Nothing could top that." She held her hand out and waggled her fingers with a wide grin on her face.

Oh, yeah, he thought, fighting back the sudden yearning to kiss her senseless. Having her back in his arms was definitely going to be the best part of the whole damn day.

The food was truly fabulous, but she'd been too keyed up to do more than just taste it. Apparently, every single man, woman and child on the island had needed to drop in to pay their respects and wish the happy couple a good life. Her face was numb from smiling at everyone.

Annie was more than a little relieved when the crowds finally dispersed and she could kick off her shoes. But then it suddenly occurred to her that she didn't know what to expect next.

Would she and Nick just settle in and be at home? She'd packed a small bag, enough to get by for tonight and tomorrow. But maybe Nick would want her to move the rest of her things into his quarters right away.

Beyond that, what else would he expect? This was their wedding night, after all.

Too embarrassed to ask him his plans, Annie sank into one of the armchairs in the dining and reception room and waited. In the back of her mind, that same low warning that Nick was pushing too hard and leaving her out of the decision making came back to taunt her.

She looked around at the rich furnishings and the expensive artwork and began to worry that this marriage didn't have a chance in hell of lasting past their child's birth. They were from such different backgrounds.

"I have asked a servant to pack a few of your things for the trip, Annie. I hope you don't mind, but I knew you wouldn't have time." Nick's mother had slipped beside her while she'd been daydreaming.

"Trip?" Had she missed an entire conversation?

Elizabeth slid an arm around her shoulders. "Don't tell me Nicholas hasn't told you about your honeymoon trip yet?"

"Honeymoon?" Annie felt like a parroting child, not quite able to keep up with the grown ups' conversation.

Elizabeth frowned and hugged her close. "You are much too sweet and accepting, dear. If that son of mine ever ends up offending you or doing something else equally stupid, I swear…"

"I'll be fine," Annie protested. "I'm not some young innocent who needs protecting. I deliberately took a job that moved me a thousand miles from home so that I could prove I can take care of myself. I'm a lot stronger and tougher than my family ever gave me credit for."

She looked up into her new mother-in-law's concerned eyes. "I can hold my own with your son, too." Patting Elizabeth's arm, Annie smiled up at her. "I love him, but I will never be anyone's doormat. Please, don't worry."

Elizabeth's eyes filled with tears. "His father and I…" She shook her head and swallowed back a sob. "You and I need to have a long talk. But not tonight. Tonight is for celebrating."

Nick appeared in the doorway from the kitchen. "The pilot is ready to leave when you are, Annie." Then he turned to his mother. "I had Annie's suitcases stowed on the plane. Is there anything else that we need to do before we go?"

Elizabeth straightened and folded her arms over her chest. "You need to start talking to your wife before you make all the decisions for her. In fact, you might want to ask her now if she even wishes to accompany you on this trip. I'm not sure *I* would if I were her."

Nick swivelled and dropped to his knees beside her with a look of pure horror on his face. "Annie…I forgot I hadn't told you. Dammit. I sincerely apologize. This is the surprise I mentioned before. It's supposed to be fun for you…for both of us. I didn't mean to…"

"Shush," Annie whispered as she put her fingertips to his lips. "Don't panic. I admit it would've been nice to be consulted about my own honeymoon trip, but let's not start out our married lives with regret. Anything you want to do will be okay with me."

Nick heaved a relieved sigh. "One of my college

roommates owns an exclusive mountainside resort on the Mexican Riviera. The honeymoon bungalow is spectacular, with its own private pool and sauna, right at the edge of a cliff where sky meets ocean. We can dance until dawn with movie stars and royalty on the resort's beach. Then we'll sleep the day away in total luxury without interference from anyone, completely on our own, if that's what we want to do. It'll be perfect."

Annie could see his desire to make love to her written all over Nick's features. She knew what that look meant because she'd been having the exact same desires. The memory of their past passion was still clear and sharp in both her mind and her body after all these weeks.

But now that she was faced with their wedding night—and the expected result—she wasn't entirely sure that she was ready to experience all those intense feelings again. Not just yet. And especially not when he'd been so overbearing about everything.

If she simply fell into his arms tonight, how would she ever be able to hold her own with him again? Making love to Nick made her too vulnerable. Too needy for more of him than he wanted to give.

With a yellow fog of panic about to choke her, Annie came to the decision that she needed more time before she and Nick could be intimate again. Time to make herself strong enough so that she could be with him and not be destroyed by loving a man who refused to love her in return.

A few days…or weeks ought to do it.

With the decision to wait set in her mind, Annie felt much better about the trip. "The place sounds just fine,

Nick." She stood up and felt the strength returning to her body. "I'm ready to go when you are."

Neither of them said much on the three-hour plane trip to the resort. Nick apologized several times for forgetting to tell her where they were going. The surprise trip didn't need forgiving. The assumption that he could make all the decisions did. But Annie wasn't sure yet how to discuss it with him.

In fact, the two of them needed to do a lot of talking. Since she'd made the decision that they should take it slow and get to know each other better before they made love again, Annie felt much more in control. That was one decision that she could make on her own.

Of course, she wanted Nick to agree with her. But she still wasn't sure how to approach the subject. The man had been her boss up until this morning. Their relationship would have to go through a lot of changes.

When they arrived at the resort, they were driven up the side of a mountain in a golf cart. The setting sun hung out over the ocean like a great orange fireball, readying itself for a night's dip in the cool water below.

She'd thought that Nick's island was exotic and different. But this place, with its lush foliage and spicy Latin music filling the evening air, was beyond her imaginings.

Entering the bungalow with Nick, Annie had to catch herself before she made a foolish and naive remark about how spectacular the place was. Floor-to-ceiling picture windows looked out at the edge of the cliff toward the Pacific Ocean.

Sixty-foot pine trees, strangely shaped rocks peak-

ing up through the surf from the ocean's floor, and
rocky paths lit by torches winding through dense foliage down to the main resort could be seen out the fantastic walls of glass. The sights were breathtaking, but
she didn't want to appear to be too unsophisticated.
She had to watch herself until she figured out how to
get along in his world.

She spun around to see if Nick was as stunned by the
sight as she was. But he had casually wandered over to
a heavily laden table, set up in front of a fireplace and
loaded down with various foods.

"Are you hungry?" he asked. "This is quite a spread,
but if you're still full from the reception, I'll ask them
to take it away."

"No," she said, suddenly famished. She moved to the
table and stared down at mounds of fresh fruit, a tall pile
of cold peeled shrimp and a heaping bowl of guacamole
spiked with fresh tomatoes.

She didn't want to seem too anxious. "I could eat
something," she said offhandedly as she reached for a
charred chicken wing.

Nick picked up a corn tortilla chip and popped it into
his mouth. Then he frowned as he watched Annie dain-
tily pick over the food. It wasn't like her to be so ten-
tative and it was starting to grate on his nerves.

"You didn't say how you liked the bungalow and the
view," he asked as he scooped up a shrimp. "Are you
happy with my choice of a honeymoon destination?"

She shrugged a shoulder and nibbled on a cheese
quesadilla. "I suppose."

Her totally uncharacteristic nonchalant attitude was
more than he could take. "What the hell is the matter

with you? Are you still angry about me making this decision alone?"

Annie lifted her chin and narrowed her eyes. "Why are *you* mad all of a sudden? Have I done something wrong?"

Frustrated, he blew out a breath. "Of course not. But you're so quiet. It's not like you."

A flame of blush pink ran up her neck and reached her cheeks. "I'm trying to be more sophisticated. I want to fit into your life."

He reached for her then and took her by the shoulders. "Don't... Don't try to be someone else. Christina was sophisticated and too quiet. I never knew what she was thinking. It was...difficult."

Annie frowned and lowered her eyes.

"Hell," he muttered, annoyed with himself now. "I didn't mean to upset you by talking about Christina. I promise never to do it in the future." Christina would only suffer in the comparison, he knew.

Nick steadied his voice and drew Annie to his chest. "Just be yourself, sweetheart. And always tell me exactly what you think and feel," he whispered in her ear.

Annie was so warm in his arms that he immediately sank back into the purple haze of desire that had become his perpetual companion. He could hear her breathing change, becoming more shallow as he felt her nipples peak against his chest, burning spots right through his clothes and tantalizing him.

Suddenly, he wanted nothing more than to be here with this sensual woman. He closed his eyes and breathed in the light scents of rose water and cinnamon, the smells surrounding her that had always left him hard and aching.

He leaned back, lifted her chin and kissed her. But as their lips touched, his brain exploded with dizzying yearnings. Too long denied the erotic sensations that being with her caused inside him, he poured all the years of loneliness and grief into this one kiss.

She moaned softly against his lips as their tongues met, tangled and sought the liquid warmth of each other. Briefly, he thought he'd caught a strange sensation of belonging. Of rightness and strength.

But as soon her lush body pressed against him, burned into his thighs and more importantly leaned heavily against his groin, he blocked out everything else. The guilty pleasures he found with Annie made him forget all about promises, honor and trust.

Annie's brain was in turmoil. She'd wanted this kiss, this closeness, more than she thought possible. Dreams of the passion they'd created together had kept her up at night. But she'd made that promise to herself to wait, and she knew it would be the smart thing to do.

Nick's hands roamed over her back and up her sides to the underside of her breasts. A shock of electricity zinged through her veins. But the intensity of need it stirred up only served to remind her again that this was too soon.

Was he thinking of the times the two of them had shared the same way she was? Or was he remembering what he had shared with his wife so long ago? And was he wishing…?

Annie pulled back from the kiss and touched his chest. "Nick, wait, please."

He opened his eyes but she could tell it cost him. Trying to focus on her face, he mumbled, "Wait? Why?"

"I know we're married and this may seem silly to you, but I'm worried about us rushing into another physical relationship before we get to know each other better."

"We've known each other for nearly eight months," he began dryly and dropped his hands. "And some of that 'knowing' was rather intimate. We didn't seem to have any problems in that department. What more do we need?"

"How old am I, Nick?"

"Excuse me?"

"I don't know how old you are. And it occurs to me, you don't know about me either."

"I'll be thirty next week," he told her with some hesitation and confusion.

"A Leo? I should've known. I'm a Virgo, a practical romantic. I'll be twenty-five on fifth of September.

"See?" she continued. "There are lots of things we don't know about each other yet. For instance, do you want more children after this one? I've always wanted to have four kids, two boys and two girls. It just seems like a nice, round number. And I don't know what kind of business your family runs in Alsaca. I think that might be important. I mean, what if your family is into something illegal? Not that I really think so. But…"

"Annie," he whispered with a hint of a smile. "You're rambling again. There's no need to be nervous with me. I can't say I'm terribly happy about the idea of waiting before we make love again, but I see your point. We have our whole lives. If this is that important to you, I can't see any reason for us to push."

Her shoulders slumped with relief. But as soon as she

thought she was home free, his mouth came down on hers in a restrained brush of lips and tongue. The sensual temptation of that nearly chaste kiss turned her into a mound of mush. Maybe she had been too hasty.

Nick pulled back and blinked. "Damn. What—" His voice cracked. "What do you want to do now?"

In desperation she forced her gaze from his beautiful face and tried to think. Through a window, she saw their private swimming pool, and another one of her promises flipped into her mind like the turning of a page.

"I want to go for a swim," she said with a rough voice. "Please come with me."

"Swimming?" He started to shake his head, but then apparently thought better of it. "I didn't bring a suit."

"But it's our own private pool. You don't need a suit. Just wear shorts…or maybe your underwear."

Without a word, he grinned and raised an eyebrow.

Oh, good Lord. What had she just gotten herself into?

Ten

Nick tried to put a damper on his growing needs, but it wasn't easy. Especially since Annie had changed into a new red two-piece swimming suit and was treading water in their lighted private pool—and gazing up at him expectantly.

Expectantly. Yes, that was a good idea. He could think about all the things he'd learned from the Internet over the past two days about a woman's pregnancy.

He'd done the research because he wanted an idea of what to expect. And it had been fascinating, imagining the changes that would take place in Annie's body. Fascinating and somehow arousing. Not that he needed anything more to inflame him whenever he thought about Annie—which was constantly these days.

He eased out of his shirt and pants and draped them over a deck chair. The warm summer breeze off the ocean gently caressed his skin the same way a woman's fingers might. It stirred his blood until at last he found himself biting the inside of his cheek to keep from groaning aloud.

Think, you idiot! Don't let yourself lose control, he cautioned himself. He owed Annie the honor of abiding by her wishes. And she'd probably been right about taking things slow.

Now if only he could convince his body to cooperate.

Lowering himself into the soft cocoon of warm pool water, Nick tried going over the facts of pregnancy as he'd memorized them. "A woman's body will become rounder as the months go by. Her breasts will become more sensitive…"

Hell. That wasn't the direction he wanted his thoughts to go—not now.

"Nick. Is everything okay?"

He blinked his eyes and found that Annie had swum up beside him. He could swear the heat emanating from her body was boiling him alive even from a distance of two feet away.

"Yeah. Everything's just terrific." He glanced down at her form through the backlit water and took a breath.

Her red bathing suit was just about the sexiest thing he had ever seen. Not that it was one of those thong things, but the v-neckline exposed more of her rounded curves than he needed to see at the moment.

Annie's body looked as though it had already become fuller. The need to retrace her every curve, her every line, with both his fingers and his tongue was making him crazy with desires he'd rather not have at the moment.

Still…he couldn't keep a rein on his thoughts. Would her skin also have become more sensitive this soon? Annie had been hypersensitive to his touch before. And very expressive about it too, as he remembered. How would that have changed?

He felt another sudden rush of blood, beating a path to his straining arousal. Determined to respect Annie, he ducked his head and swam to the far side of the pool. Away from the temptation.

As he touched the wall and reached for the edge, something under the water tugged at his foot. Instantly, Annie surfaced beside him, laughing with delight as bubbles foamed between the two of them. The teasing bubbles tickled his skin, and made him think of how Annie's touch had been.

Wrong. Stop that kind of thinking now, he warned himself once again. But the roar of desire was already too loud in his ears and his body refused to pay attention.

"You're really swimming," she exclaimed with a smile. "You totally rock!"

"Swimming is no big deal," he grumbled. "It's just a pool. Not the ocean."

Annie lightly shook her head and touched his arm through the water. The electric jolt of her hand on his skin set off sparkling fireworks in his mind, blinding him to promises, honor, trust. Blinded him to everything—but pure basic need.

Without a second thought he dove to the bottom, rising up underneath Annie's body in just the right position to capture her beside the pool wall. She didn't say anything, but her eyes were dancing with obvious desire. She laughed again as he moved even closer.

Desperate to pull back from the abyss of temptation, he put his wide hand against her bare stomach and tried one last time to think of their child growing inside her. Anything to stop the madness that was quickly swallowing him whole. He tried, but the soft texture of her skin made his mind fill with all the wrong images.

"Nick, please," she warned softly.

He managed one last weak smile. "Do you have a preference for a boy or a girl?"

Annie blinked and swallowed a little water. "What a crazy thing to ask right now. No, I don't care. Either one will be just fine as long as it's born healthy."

Nothing she said was sinking in. Sliding his hand up between her breasts, he traced the edge of her suit with his fingers. "The experts all say you'll become more sensitive as the days go on. Have you noticed?"

"Uh…"

With their bodies mere inches apart, she seemed to be having trouble staying afloat. He closed even that small gap between them, leaving her no space and no choice.

Slipping his knee between her legs, he let her ride his thigh and keep her head above water. He steadied them both by hanging unto the edge of the deck behind her with one hand.

But once they were stable, he made the fatal mistake of looking down at her body again. Her shimmering red suit was the last temptation and the last straw. He couldn't help himself. Some animal demand, deep in his subconscious, drove his hand to touch what he coveted.

Slowly, he edged his fingers up one strap of her suit

and tugged at the loosely tied knot behind her neck. Both red straps fell away and the whole front of the bathing suit floated down to her waist, exposing creamy breasts—all rounded and tilted upward toward him.

The skin there was whiter than he remembered. And the nipples were larger than before, pinched and so fully engorged they were purple. Amazing…and narcotic.

Not able to stand another minute just looking, Nick reached to touch a peaked tip. "When I do this, is it too tender to the touch?" He used the pad of his finger to circle the nipple, wondering at how quickly it stood up for him.

Annie made a soft sound in her throat and he glanced up to check her expression. Was she angry? Not exactly. Her eyes were closed, her nostrils flared and her breathing ragged.

She was every bit as turned on as he was, but she appeared to be fighting it desperately. As for him…he couldn't bear it another minute without…

He held his breath and bent his head under the water to flick his tongue over the tortured nipple, tasting, testing. She dug her fingers through his hair and held his head in place, letting him know how good it felt.

Without breathing—or thinking—he found his fingers sliding up her thigh and testing the elastic at her crotch. He let his forefinger slip inside the suit to touch the tender edges of his ultimate destination.

Just a little test, he thought vaguely. He would back off in one more minute.

But it was warmer to his touch there…and wetter…and sweeter.

Lifting his head again to watch her expression, he saw Annie bite her lip as he slipped his index finger inside her body. Surprised, she slid a little lower in the water. He put his arm around her protectively, holding her close to his body while he managed another finger inside her depths.

Once two fingers were inside the tightness of her body, he flexed them both. Annie moaned against his neck, driving his madness beyond any control. He was crazy with the desire to watch her come for him. Mad to see her face fill with color and pleasure.

He ripped at the material of her suit that was keeping him from his goal. It gave way and he was suddenly free to flick a thumb over her most sensitive nub.

As he lightly rubbed and plucked, he tightened his grip around her waist to hold her steady. She stilled then, and widened her glazed eyes for one second to question his intentions. But a millisecond later, her eyes rolled and closed. He felt the beginning rumbles of climax as her internal muscles tightened around his fingers.

The garbled scream came involuntarily from deep inside her gut as she grabbed for his neck. The sensations had caught her off-guard. She seemed to be fighting to hold them off and stay afloat.

"Let it happen, sweetheart," he groaned against her hair as he tightened his grip. "I'm here to keep you safe."

"Oh, God, Nick," Annie gulped.

She was shivering in his arms, and he reveled in the delicious pleasure of holding her close.

But before he could lean in for another kiss, she

reared back and smacked him in the chest as hard as she could through the water.

"Dammit." She pushed away and narrowed her eyes at him. "I thought you said you wouldn't do that tonight. You promised to give us time."

His head snapped up and he felt like she'd struck him with a lead pipe instead of lightly pushing him with her hands. Hell. What had he done?

"I'm…I'm…" he gasped as he backed away from her. What could he say? His behavior was beyond reprehensible.

So he said nothing. Just turned abruptly, swam to the other side of the pool and heaved himself out onto the deck.

"Nick, where are you going?"

"I'm sorry, okay? I'm going to take a sauna." He couldn't look at her, couldn't stop to think or apologize again.

Making a dash for the redwood sauna, he closed himself off from his inappropriate actions, then swung open the door to the familiar and heated mists of guilt and regret.

Annie was left, shivering and feeling more than miserable in the lonely pool. Thank heaven Nick had moved away when she'd first asked. Another minute or two and she would have caved, begging him to stay, to be with her and come inside her.

She grasped the pool steps with shaky hands and pulled herself heavily out of the water. It simply amazed her that with as much control as Nick usually had over his emotions, he could be so outrageously passionate and so intense when the two of them came together.

It was the intensity that scared the hell out of her. She was deathly afraid she could easily lose herself to it and to him. And she simply refused to do that—to fall totally out of control with a man who didn't love her—would never love her.

But Annie had a feeling that all the passion was a new experience for Nick, too. His gaze had been too bruised tonight when he'd realized what he'd done.

Was this much intensity just part of a normal sex life? If so, it made her wonder why Nick seemed so stunned by it.

Holding her tattered suit close to her body, Annie made a dash for the bathroom shower. As balmy as the air here was, she felt cold.

She stepped into the hot shower stream and immediately the memories of Nick touching her under the water flashed in her mind. Her body responded but she fought it.

The crazy fight between sensual and practical images in her mind made her remember the reality of her situation. She was actually a married woman, expecting Nick's child. Sooner or later she would probably have to face making love to him again.

Sooner sounded much better to her at the moment. But she had to find a way not to lose herself to him when it happened.

Annie planted her feet and set her jaw. She was strong. Strong enough to take on anything if she put her mind to it.

Perhaps she'd gone about this the wrong way. Maybe

if they had more sex, not less, the intensity would naturally wear off and then it wouldn't terrify her so much.

Great idea. Now, how could she tell Nick that she'd changed her mind?

She stepped from the shower and wrapped herself in a huge, super luxurious towel. Suddenly, she was so tired she couldn't think straight. It had been such a long day.

In two seconds flat she'd made her way to the king-size bed and slipped between the sheets. She needed some sleep. As she laid her head on the pillow, Annie briefly wondered how Nick was doing in the sauna.

The last thing in her thoughts before she closed her eyes and fell sound asleep was the hope that maybe tonight she would dream up a way to let him know she'd changed her mind. Later when she awoke, everything would be okay.

The very next thing Annie knew was when the thin gray light of predawn crept into the room and plucked at her eyelids. She blinked open her eyes, shifted her stiff body and rolled on her back.

It took a minute to orient herself to the room, to the place, to the bed. The bed. She was clearly not alone in this huge bed.

Turning over, she saw Nick, laying on his side and facing her. He was asleep, his breathing slow and deep.

When she cleared her eyes and focused on him, she nearly groaned aloud. The man was so handsome it hurt to look at him, even fast asleep with his chin stubbled in a morning beard and his fabulous gold and silver hair tumbling lightly over the pillow.

But as she studied him a little closer, she noticed that his forehead was creased in a frown and he held his shoulders high and tight in a fighter's stance. She reached out to touch his cheek. He shouldn't have to look so tense in his sleep. Had she done that to him?

Or was he still fighting his memories of a dead wife, even in his dreams?

Her heart lurched. She'd been selfish to hold him off last night. What had he done so wrong, anyway? He'd given her passion and tenderness and asked nothing for himself.

And hadn't she told herself that she would be the one to heal this lonely man? Fine way for her to make a lost soul pay for being noble. Boy, did she ever know how to show a man she loved him. Not.

Well, today was a new beginning. The first full day of their married lives.

Tentatively, she let her fingers glide down from his face to touch his wide, strong shoulders. There must be some way for her to release the tension in them.

Trailing her hand down his arm then across his chest, she gave herself permission to follow the ridges and muscles to the smattering of hair in the center of his chest. Warm. The hair was a soft mat of fur covering warm skin and a steadily beating heart.

Nick stirred slightly, threw off his light covering and rolled on his back. But he didn't awaken. Annie inched closer, longing to feel a tiny bit of the warmth of his body seeping into her own.

But now that he was uncovered, the temptation to run her palm down the flat of his belly, following the lines of hair to points beyond the waistband of his undershorts proved overwhelming. She felt a little wicked touching him as he slept, but she was fascinated and delighted.

His muscles jumped under her hand. And when she eased her fingers below his waistband, she noticed his shaft stirring, lifting, coming to life and growing solid.

Her fingers began to itch, craving the feel of him. Another inch and…

Nick's hand snaked out and grabbed her wrist, pulling her hand away from its destination. "Don't," he growled. "Teasing is unbecoming in a married woman. Don't push me too far."

"I wasn't…I…I've changed my mind, Nick. I think we should…now. I mean, we're married and…"

"Annie," he whispered. "I thought a lot about what you said last night, and you were right. We need more time. I want us to be friends first. I want us to know everything about each other before we lose ourselves to the sexual side of each other again. It's the right way to begin a life together."

"But…"

"Was I crowding you in this bed?" he interrupted. "When we get back to the island, I'll set myself up in the guest room next to the master bedroom if you need the bed to yourself. Until…we're ready."

"No. That's okay," she murmured quickly. The disappointment raged in her body, while her head told her that this was all for the best. "You weren't crowding me. I think I can manage to be adult enough to stay on my own side of an oversized king bed."

He brightened and sat up. "Are you hungry?"

She lowered her chin, not able to look into his brilliant blue eyes, afraid that he would see her disappointment and need. "I guess so."

His fingers touched her cheek, slid under her chin

and lifted it. "Annie, you must know I want you. That hasn't changed. Let's just give each other a break. We'll know when the time is right. We have our whole lives."

"Okay, Nick. If you think so."

She'd agreed because his argument sounded a lot more rational than she was feeling at the moment. But deep down a tiny bud of anger blossomed in her gut. Once more he had controlled what they did and had made the decision without her. Which hurt, even if she *had* been the first one to make the stupid suggestion.

"Come on," he chided her. "Let's eat and then I'll call the pilot and we'll go home. A honeymoon bungalow is no place for two people who are just trying to get to know each other. We'll be better off returning to work and getting on with out lives."

The thought of going back to see the dolphins made her happy. She had a place there and friends and was in charge.

"Yes, let's do that." She turned over and began to crawl out of the bed.

"Oh, and Annie…" he said, putting a hand on her shoulder.

"Yes?"

"Three. And it's heavy construction and real estate finance."

"What?" She shook her head and turned to see him grinning at her.

"I've always wanted three kids," he said with a chuckle. "Two girls and a boy. And for six generations my family has specialized in financing and building roads, bridges and dams all over the world."

She couldn't help giggling at his strained attempt to

make friends. The damn man was just too adorable to stay mad.

"Well, it's not everything," he said, suddenly sober. "But it's a start. Maybe this will turn out to be easier than we think."

And quicker, Annie prayed. Please God make them be "friends" in a hurry.

Eleven

The next two weeks became the slowest fourteen days of her entire life. Annie was beginning to question every decision she'd ever made.

It wouldn't be so frustrating if she and Nick were actually becoming friends. Or, if she could figure out a way to get him to cross the invisible line he'd drawn down the middle of their bed.

But no… From the minute they had returned to the island, Nick went right back to working sixteen-hour days on his rebuilding-after-the-hurricane campaign.

He'd managed to finish the construction on the guest quarters in a week. Her old suite of rooms was already redecorated. But stood empty. The same as her bed.

Currently, Nick was striving to build new housing to replace some of the islanders' shacks, lost to the hurricane. He managed to leave the house before she awoke every morning and didn't return until Annie was fast asleep at night. They barely spoke to each other.

Sighing, Annie sat on the cliff steps and emptied the sand from her deck shoes. She admired him for being so industrious and responsible. But she would give anything to get another glimpse of the private Nick. The one who could be so intense it was scary.

She felt like she was drying up from loneliness. Thirsty for a smile, a laugh, a touch and a kiss.

In some ways, though, her life was better than ever. She should be thankful that the morning sickness seemed to have released its hold on her. And she was exceedingly grateful her health was good, at least.

She'd always imagined that she would have no trouble being pregnant. She came from good Irish stock whose women popped out babies and went back to work in the potato fields the very next day. Her mother delivered seven kids with ease, and two of her sisters had so far had four children between them without hardly batting an eyelash.

Annie took her vitamins and ate right, if way too much, and exercised regularly. She felt wonderful.

And she was miserable.

She hadn't yet told her family that she was expecting. Though two days ago, she'd finally screwed up enough nerve to tell her mother that she and Nick were married.

Maeve Riley's long stunned silence after the announcement had said everything. But Annie still had to listen for another hour while her mother cried and stormed and tried everything in her repertoire to make Annie feel guilty for not inviting the family and for not having the ceremony in a church.

Annie did feel guilty, sort of. And she would try to work up an apology someday in the future when she wasn't so darned desperate to get her husband back onto her side of the bed. Really she would.

"Hello, Annie," Elizabeth's voice said from behind her. "Are you all done for the day at such an early hour? You're not feeling sick are you?"

Annie turned to her mother-in-law and grinned. "The research team has everything quite well in hand. There's not much for me to do anymore except keep the books."

"That's good," Elizabeth said with a smile. "Would you like to go shopping with me, then? We could hop over to St. Thomas for the afternoon, if you'd like."

Shoving her shoes back on, Annie stood. "No thanks." She took her mother-in-law's arm and leaned in to whisper conspiratorially. "Can you keep a secret?"

"From Nick? Perhaps. It would depend on the nature of the secret."

"It's nothing bad. I'm not in any trouble or anything." She made up her mind to let Elizabeth in on the secret pleasure she had discovered recently. She'd been dying to tell someone.

"I'm…" There was nothing to do but come out with it. "Well, I've been taking sailing lessons."

Elizabeth raised her eyebrows. "I take it my son is unaware of these lessons."

"I haven't told him," Annie mumbled as she felt the shame flame her face. "I knew he wouldn't like the idea.

"But I'm finding I love everything about sailing," she rushed on. "The thrill of turning into the wind and feeling it catch the sails. The speed as you cut through the water. It's all wonderful."

Elizabeth smiled but sadness filled her eyes. "You sound just like Nicholas did when he was ten and first discovered his own love of sailing."

Annie was petrified that Elizabeth would tell Nick her secret. It would be a major setback to making her husband a friend. And to finally having him want her again.

"Don't tell him just yet, please?" she begged. "Nick is so…uh…controlling. He'd never let me continue, and it gives me so much pleasure." And at some point, when she was more of an expert, Annie wanted to convince Nick to come sailing with her. She knew she could help him through it.

Her mother-in-law reached out a hand and tenderly pushed a wind-blown strand of hair back from her face. "Come inside with me a moment. I'd like to tell you something."

When they were seated in the pool house's front room, Elizabeth took her hand across the tiny table. "I think I owe you an explanation about my son. About what drives him to be who he is."

The older woman sounded so serious, for a moment Annie was afraid to hear what she had to say. But she sat still and waited.

"When I was about your age," Elizabeth began. "I met a man who was dashing and exciting…but unfortunately had no family and absolutely no money or prospects. My family did not approve, but I was in love.

"I deliberately lied to my young man and let myself become pregnant with his child so my family would have to let us marry," she continued.

Annie drew her hand away and began to shake her head.

"I know that's not what you did, dear. I'm not accusing you of anything." Elizabeth frowned. "In my own roundabout way, I'm trying to make you understand…about my husband…Nicholas's father…and about their relationship.

"You see, my husband cared for me, but he always felt that my family hated him…thought he was beneath them. It wasn't true, but there was nothing I could do to change his mind. He accepted a job from my father and set to work proving he was worthy of being in the family."

Annie sat back in her chair and tried to listen with her heart instead of her mind.

"He worked such long hours that I never saw him. I think he was always a little perturbed that I had lied to him as well. Whatever it was that drove him, by the time Nicholas arrived, we were like strangers. My husband's every waking minute had become devoted to the business."

Annie didn't like the sound of this story and found she was holding her breath.

Elizabeth sighed. "I'm ashamed to say, Nicholas never knew love at home. Oh, I told him I loved him, surely. But he never saw how love should be between a man a woman. His mother and father were merely civil to one another.

"My dashing lover had become a controlling, unemotional stranger to his family," Elizabeth said sadly. "As Nicholas grew, he tried to find a way to get under his father's shell, but he never could break through." Elizabeth's eyes welled up. "We both tried."

"Why did you stay with a man like that?"

"I loved him," she answered simply. "What's more, I always felt he needed me somehow. And…I suppose I have never forgiven myself for the trickery. I'd thought I'd done it out of love, but I was really being selfish. It wasn't his fault our lives turned out the way they did."

Annie dashed the tears off her cheeks. "I'm glad you told me. I understand Nick a little better now."

"No, dear heart. That wasn't my main point." Elizabeth took her hand again. "I meant this story to be a warning…a lesson in what not to do. Nothing good can come from lies. And the worst thing you can do in your marriage is to allow Nicholas to become a controlling stranger. That will be his first impulse, it's what he's always known."

She leaned over and placed a soft kiss against Annie's forehead. "My son is warm and generous and full of love he doesn't yet know how to show. If you allow him to keep it bottled inside, the two of you will never find happiness together.

"Don't make my mistakes, Annie," she whispered. "Shake some good sense into your dashing lover. Before it's too late for you both."

Nick raised his face to the sun and laughed, really laughed for the first time in years. What a glorious day.

Racing his Jeep along the north shore road in the bright golden haze of late afternoon sun, he headed toward the marina. Not entirely positive why Annie had called and asked him to meet her at that place, he was absolutely sure of her motives. He knew she had something to tell him.

And he couldn't wait to see her face when he told her

about his new surprise in return. They were about to have the breakthrough in their relationship that he'd been praying for. Finally.

His darling Annie had actually called her family and told them about their marriage. He knew because her mother had called him yesterday and asked to come for a visit. The plane he'd sent to bring her family would be arriving within the next half hour.

Annie. She must have decided that she was actually happy to be married to him and intended to stay married. He'd begun to wonder if that would ever happen. The fear that she would leave him had kept him frozen and away from her. He couldn't bear the thought of losing her.

A glint of sunlight bounced off the deep blue of the ocean and suddenly sent him spiraling back in time to another day when he'd been traveling this road to meet his wife at the marina. The worst day of his life.

The memories came fast and strong, blinding him to his current situation and putting him right back there.

Nick had been trying for days to hide his anger at Christina. He could feel the bile forming in his throat even now. But on this sunny day things would be different.

He would demand that Christina learn to sail, it was the one thing that still gave him pleasure and he was positive it would be the one thing they could do together that would repair the marriage. And they must repair the marriage. She simply could not leave him.

His father would never approve of a divorce, would never forgive him if Christina left. Their marriage had been the one thing that he'd done to win his father's favor. To have even a small sense that his father really cared.

As Nick drove around the last bend in the road, the marina and boats came into full view. The sight of them brought him back to the present with a thud.

This was the last place he would've come voluntarily. He hated seeing the boats. It gave him a niggling sense of foreboding to think of meeting Annie here. But he tried to push aside his old misgivings and forget the pain.

Today was the day he and Annie would finally come together as man and wife. There was no time for old ghosts.

He caught his first sight of her, and his breath stuck in his throat. Annie was standing on the deck of a sloop, and she was turning the boom and dropping the sail.

No! He pulled into the parking space, jammed the transmission into Park and made a dash to the dock.

"Annie," he yelled, as he ran up next to the boat. "Get off of there. What the hell do you think you're doing? Come away, now!"

She turned, blinked a couple of times and finally climbed out of the boat. Walking up the dock toward him, she smiled but the look in her eyes was wary and vulnerable.

"Hello, Nick," she said calmly. "Thank you for coming."

He grabbed her by the arm and dragged her down the dock, farther away from the boats. "Why are you here? You know how I feel about boats and sailing."

Annie tugged her arm free of his grip and stopped walking. "I've been taking sailing lessons. I didn't want to hide it from you anymore."

When he began to protest, she interrupted him, "I love sailing, Nick. It makes me feel so free, like a bird, skimming over the water. I know now why you loved it, and I was hoping…"

She took a breath and straightened her shoulders. "Despite your old fears and guilt, I thought maybe you would consider going back to it so we could sail together. I'll be with you, to help you find your way back."

He couldn't talk, couldn't breathe. Just stared at her. He remained mute and shook his head in shock.

"Your mother tells me you were once the best sailor in the Caribbean. Teach me to be the best, too."

The panic doubled him over and he put his arm across his waist to keep from collapsing. "My God, Annie. How could you ask such a thing of me? I thought we were getting to know each other, but this shows me you know nothing about me at all."

"Nick… Please…" She reached out and put a tender, warm hand on his arm.

The fierce longing for her that stayed constantly buried right under his skin drove him over an edge. He dragged her closer and took her lips with a force that might've surprised him any other time. After all these weeks of denying themselves, they responded to each other with shivering, sobbing passion.

He didn't care where they were. Didn't care who might be watching. He only cared that Annie clung to him, pressed her breasts against his chest and swivelled her hips against his groin, begging him silently for what they both needed so desperately.

"Nick!" A bellowing voice came from over his shoulder. "It's great to see you down here again."

Annie froze, and Nick raised his head in a daze. "Hello, Bellamy," he managed. He had to get them both away from here to be alone. "If you'll excuse us, my wife and I need to talk. I'll catch up with you another time."

Dragging Annie by the hand, Nick put them both in his Jeep and took off. He didn't stop driving until the marina was far behind them. Then he pulled off the road and idled the engine.

When he turned to Annie, her expression was unfocused and dazed. It made his heart flip over with a thump, his stomach sour, and his own eyes blur with a sheen of tears.

"Annie, please listen to me," he said roughly. "I'm not ready for this yet. And…and it makes me sick to think of you going out on the sea right now. Don't… don't…"

She took his hand. "Right now? Is it because of the baby? Please don't be afraid for us. I'm healthy and strong. Everything will be fine."

That wasn't what he'd meant, but come to think of it, she was going to be a mother and had no business out on the ocean. "Aren't you even a little afraid?"

"Well, sure. Most mothers are scared their first time. You wouldn't believe the stories you hear. But that's normal." She gazed up into his eyes and the look she gave him was soft and tender. "Okay, okay. I won't sail again until after the baby is born. But then will you please reconsider going with me?"

Pleased that she'd given in, even though it was not in the way he would've preferred, Nick lifted her hand and placed a kiss in her palm. What was one little fib, if it meant they would be together again?

"I promise to think about it again…after the baby is born," he murmured then lifted his head. "Now, let's go back to the main house to change for dinner. I have a fantastic surprise for you later."

Annie laughed and threw her head back. "I hope you mean much later…in our bed."

"Yes," he began with his own grin covering his face. That would be good too. "This will be a night to remember."

Annie fussed with the button on her new fushia shirt. Not even three months pregnant yet and nothing fit her right. Elizabeth had brought her several new outfits with elastic waistbands and blouses that didn't need to be tucked in. But the shirt she'd wanted to wear tonight was already too tight around the bustline.

She quickly changed into the pretty poppy colored outfit that had no buttons and checked herself in the mirror. It was a great color on her, and she sure hoped Nick would like it. This afternoon, in his arms he hadn't seemed to take any notice of her burgeoning figure at all.

It felt so good for them to be talking again. She was glad she'd gotten the nerve to tell him about her sailing, even though she hadn't been able to change his mind. It was better if things were out in the open.

Just maybe their marriage had a chance of making it, after all. She loved him enough for both of them. And if tonight they were going to become lovers again, everything was bound to be okay.

Her mind was filled with music and flowers as she danced down the hallway toward the kitchen. Succulent smells wafted toward her and she began to hum. All was right with the world.

Turning the last corner, Annie was secure knowing what to expect. But just then two strange figures appeared, following Nick down the hall from the guest suite. Had he invited company?

Two more steps and the strangers took form in the kitchen's light. Familiar forms. Beloved faces looked up at her and smiled. Annie froze and clutched at her chest.

"Ma! Da! I can't believe you're here!" She closed the gap between them and let her parents wrap her in loving embraces.

"Surprised, *dervla?*" Her mother hugged her tight. "Nicholas sent his plane for us. I would've thought…"

It took Annie a full minute to realize her mother had backed up a step and was staring down at her belly and then up to her bustline. The panic hit hard, with a swift kick to the butt. Too late to run now.

"A baby, Annie?" Her mother's expression was pained.

"Yes, Ma," Annie gulped as she lifted her chin to take her medicine. "Another grandchild is on the way."

Her mother grinned. "Well, no wonder you got married so fast." Maeve rolled her eyes toward the heavens with an exaggerated sigh. "Thank the good Lord."

Twelve

A half hour later, after introductions and tons of tears, the newly combined family members were called to the dining room. Annie hadn't said much so far. She was too nervous about what her mother would have to say when they had a moment alone. Annie knew she was in for a lecture.

But all through dinner Nick was the most gracious host. He smiled at her from across the table and even winked once when no one else was looking. His mother, Elizabeth, had been a calming influence as usual.

The food was wonderful. But though it was one of the chef's best efforts, Annie couldn't eat more than a bite.

Elizabeth suggested they take coffee and dessert out on the patio, as the balmy night was a perfect temperature and the sky was a star-filled spectacular. She spoke to the chef and led the way. Following along behind Elizabeth, Nick and Annie's father were still caught up in a discussion of the island's police force.

Annie's mother rose, moved to her side and slipped an arm around her daughter's shoulders, whispering in her ear, "You really found your Prince Charming, *dervla*. He's so handsome, just like in your storybooks when you were a girl. And so pleasant. He will make you a good husband."

Stunned, Annie couldn't speak. Where was the lecture about marrying out of the church? Where were the hurt feelings about not being at her youngest daughter's wedding?

"I'm proud of you Annie," her mother continued. "It's plain to see you have at last become an adult. For so long I've fretted that my baby would forever be letting the family bully her. But you went out into the world and made a life by yourself, and now you're doing all the right things with a man you obviously adore."

Annie's mother hugged her close and kissed her cheek. "I only wish you could've done your living closer to home," she stopped and sighed. "But I see that you had to do things in your own way and in your own time."

"Oh, Ma," Annie said with a hitch in her voice. "I love you so much." Something clicked in her head then and she knew her mother was right. She would never again let anyone control her choices. Annie Riley Scoville was an adult, a wife and about to be a mother.

As they walked arm in arm out to join the others, Annie's heart swelled with love for Nick. She couldn't wait to show him how much she loved him by getting her hands on him. In fact, she didn't want to wait another minute. In new adult mode, she was ready to make her own choices.

Nick stood next to the patio table, watching Annie and her mother walking toward him. His mouth watered at the very first sight of his wife, with her hair slightly tousled by the soft ocean breeze and her blazing green eyes looking in his direction with a yearning that he'd been feeling, too.

He'd had a moment of concern before dinner when Annie first spotted her parents, worrying that she would be furious that he hadn't warned her of their visit. But that didn't seem to be a problem. She'd laughed at his dinner conversation and gave him secret smiles. It had been all he could do not to drag her away before the first course.

Darling Annie, he groaned silently. She was the delightfully colorful and terribly erotic love of his life.

Everything went still. His heart waited for his brain to catch up. *Love?* Was that what this heavy feeling in his chest meant? If so, it was the first time in his life he'd ever really been in love.

It scared him, panicked him. What was love? The only thing he could think of at the moment was that he would die if she left him. He could not live without her. Would not.

But Annie wouldn't do that to him. She wouldn't walk away as Christina had done—not his Annie. And he intended to keep her safe and sound permanently.

"Uh, Nick?" Annie said softly as she walked up beside him at the table. "Could I have a word with you before the coffee is served? Please?"

She glanced down and refused to look at him. Was she angry? His mind was racing trying to come with excuses, but he couldn't concentrate. He loved her. Dear Lord, he couldn't breath with just the thought of it.

He managed a nod and she turned, quickly making her way toward his old office. He followed silently behind her. But he couldn't feel his feet touching the floor. If she was mad, he would just have to find some way around it.

All he could think about was having her back in his arms later tonight. He would tell her he loved her then and she would say she loved him too and they would show each other how much they cared—all night long.

Annie waited for him just inside the office door. He moved past her, longing to take her in his arms. But he kept silent until she closed and locked the door behind him.

"Annie," he began roughly and reached a hand out to beg her to come to him—or maybe to forgive him and love him.

She made a tiny squeak, like she couldn't manage anything else, and ran straight into his arms. He staggered under her assault, for a second. But the feel of her next to his chest—the warmth of her body and her spicy scent of cinnamon—overwhelmed his conscious mind and let his subconscious desires take charge.

"Nick. Nick," she moaned. "I need you so badly. I can't stand waiting another minute. Please." She was crying now, he could feel her tears against his neck.

"Easy, love," he said, but his body was screaming for

him to rush. Fully aroused and suddenly desperate, he orientated himself in a second and backed them both up to the desk.

Cupping her bottom, he held their bodies together and let her feel the depth of his desire. Then he bent his head and took her mouth, ravaging her with open-mouthed kisses and tangling tongues.

Annie reached between them and placed her hand firmly over his zipper. He gasped, stopped breathing, then frantically tore at her slacks and panties, dragging them down her legs.

She was just as fierce, fighting his zipper and trying to free him into her hands.

Nick backed up to the edge of the desk, balancing himself as Annie kicked her garments aside and inched between his thighs, concentrating on getting her hands on his body. At last, she sobbed his name and gently caressed his flesh. With great tenderness, she ran her fingers up and down his shaft.

"You can't know how good that feels," he moaned. I've wanted you again so badly. I haven't been able to think of anything else."

But before he could drag her closer and before he realized her intentions, Annie dropped to her knees between his legs and put her curious tongue where her fingers had just been. The electric jolt stopped his heart as she tasted, sucked and licked him freely.

Without taking her mouth away from its pleasure, she looked up into his eyes, gazing at him with such intimate emotions that Nick thought he would lose it right there.

He took her firmly by the shoulders and pulled her

up his body. "I can't…" he gasped. "Maybe later. It's been so long."

Annie threw back her head, laughed and climbed on the desk and into his lap. Her eyes were dark, her hands were everywhere at once. She fit herself down on him and wrapped her legs around his waist. He had never seen anyone so beautiful or so lost in passion. She was giving him almost unbearable pleasure.

Rearing back, Annie impaled herself more deeply on him. Warm and tight, he fit inside her perfectly. They were meant to be together forever. It was as certain as the dawn. Nothing else could ever matter this much.

"I love you," she moaned and dug her fingers into his shoulders.

She pulled her hips up, then jammed them back down against him. He could feel the circles of her climax beginning and it was the last clear thought he had.

The world dissolved in a haze of heat and stars. In the distance he could hear someone yelling, but maybe that was Annie…or him. He wondered for a second if they had both spun right off the earth. He couldn't be sure of anything.

Except—he loved her.

Annie lay cuddled against Nick's broad chest and tried to regulate her breathing. It didn't matter that her parents were waiting for them only a few yards away. It didn't matter that she had never done anything so daring before in her whole life.

All that mattered was that Nick wanted her. He had been as desperate for her as she was for him. And she was the one who had controlled what they did. It was freeing…exhilarating. She had wanted something and had taken it.

"Are you okay?" Nick asked quietly.

"Mmm." Was all she could manage at the moment.

"Do you think we ought to try to go back outside?" His voice was hoarse, his words shaky. "Maybe we can have a quick cup of coffee and then claim we're tired. We could beg to be excused early."

She kept silent for a moment, listening to his heart beating frantically under her cheek. He wanted her again, right now. What a fantastic thought.

"Annie…" He relaxed his grip and let her slowly slide to her feet. "We have to go back out there now. But we'll have all night—later."

She was light-headed and her body still hummed, but she tried to bring a little clarity to her mind. Nick helped to find her slacks and panties, then he straightened his own clothes as she redressed.

Her parents. They had to deal with her parents to-night.

When they both felt they were presentable, Nick slipped his arm tightly around her waist to keep her steady and they headed down the hall.

"I'm glad you weren't upset with me about your parents' surprise visit," Nick said after he cleared his throat.

"I'm sure my mother invited herself," Annie told him. "She can be very overbearing. I'm just amazed she isn't foaming at the mouth about us not having a church wedding."

"She was," Nick said with a laugh and tossed his head. "Until I told her we were planning to have another big church wedding later this fall. She was thrilled to know I intended to pay for all of it and wanted to fly the whole family to Alsaca for the reception. I think she likes me."

Annie stopped walking. Her heart stopped. The world stopped. Had all the air been taken from the room?

"What did you say?" she heard herself ask distantly.

"Your mother likes me?"

Annie swung around to narrow her eyes at him. "You told my mother we would have a church wedding? Without asking me?" She tried to keep her voice steady but a reddish haze had enveloped her and she couldn't focus.

"Of course." Nick's voice had grown wary, but he still didn't realize how deadly serious this was. "What's wrong with that? We're already married. You said you loved me. It's no big deal if we get married again for your family."

"No," she said as the cold began to numb her body. Icy fingers of doubt and pain drew circles around her heart.

"No?" Nick echoed and reached for her. "Why…?"

Annie backed away from his grasp, out of his reach. "You'll never change, will you Nick?" She could feel the tears threatening, but willed them down. "Everything will always have to be your way. You must have all the control."

She saw the fury and the fear fill his eyes. "What are you talking about?" he choked out. "Grow up, Annie. You're my wife. You're supposed to love me, not question me."

His words tore a bigger hole in her heart. Not only

would he never love her, but nothing she could ever do would make a difference to him. His childhood examples had affected him forever. She'd never had a chance.

She slashed her hand over her face, trying to push aside the tears. "I'm sorry, Nick. I thought I could make a life with you, but now I know it won't work between us."

"What?" He moved fast and gripped her by the arms. "What are you saying?"

The tears were running freely now and Annie had to swallow twice to talk. "I'll go pack a few things and move back out to the pool house tonight. We can talk more about details tomorrow. I need to get my thoughts together."

The look on his face ripped her in two. "You're leaving me? You can't. I won't let you." His voice cracked and he dropped his hands to his sides.

Annie had to turn her back to him, otherwise she would've fallen at his feet in a heap. But she had to be the adult here. "Make my excuses to the family, please."

With those words, she took off running. Afraid to look back yet desperate for him to say something to make her want to stay. But in her soul, she knew there was nothing that would ever make things right between them now.

"Oh Nicholas," he heard his mother say through the fog in his brain. "I'm so sorry. I tried to help guide your life in a different direction, but…"

"What the hell are you talking about, Mother?" He knew she'd been a big help for the last hour since Annie had walked away, leaving him stunned and confused.

She'd settled Annie in the pool house for the night. And she'd also managed to calm Annie's parents and shepherded them into the guest suite with soothing words.

But since then, Elizabeth hadn't been making any sense.

She gripped his shoulders and tried to shake him, but he was so much bigger than his mother that it didn't have much effect. He knew what the gesture meant, however.

"Listen to me, son," she said through gritted teeth. "You love that girl. You may not know it, but…"

"Yes, I do know it," he interrupted. "It finally hit me earlier tonight."

"Then, for God's sake, why would you treat her that way? Why would you hurt someone you love?"

"Hurt her? Don't be absurd. What *are* you saying?"

His mother dropped her hands and sighed. "Are you so blind? Have you finally lost all of yourself and turned completely into your father?"

He narrowed his eyes at her, and lifted his chin. "What does my father have to do with Annie?"

The tears filled his mother's eyes. "You've become just like him. Without even noticing, you are the same controlling, selfish man you feared and desperately tried to please while growing up."

"Me? What have I done? I only wanted to do the best for my wife. I wanted to keep her safe and happy."

"And what about her wishes, Nicholas? Did you once think to consult her about what she really wanted?"

"But…"

"It's the same thing that you did to Christina," his

mother broke in. "You thought she needed you to control her life, but she was almost as strong inside as Annie. Christina didn't die because you forced her to do something against her wishes. She wanted to be near the ocean. She made her own choices."

He could feel his cheeks flaming with the anger and the pain. Why did she have to dredge this all up now? Wasn't his current situation bad enough?

"It was your guilt about not being able to father a child that colored your memory of the relationship with Christina. Annie is a strong woman. You cannot control her whole life.

"Stop and take a look at what you are becoming. Do you want your children to think of you the same way you thought of your father?" she asked with a low, sad sigh.

A sudden image of the face of his and Annie's child, looking up at him with his own big, hopeless eyes, blinked into his mind. But he couldn't allow himself to think of that, not when everything looked so impossible with Annie.

"Thank you for your concern, Mother," he said in a more formal tone than necessary. "But I won't discuss this."

He turned and walked away, suddenly more tired than he'd ever been in his whole life. Without paying much attention to the direction his feet were taking him, Nick found himself back in his old office. The place where he and Annie had first come together—and where they had come together tonight for perhaps the last time.

Nick collapsed into his old chair, and realized he was

surrounded by things that reminded him of Annie. Her books on the desktop. Her scent still in the air. He even imagined he could feel her warmth in the leather under him.

How could this happen to him? To find the one passion, the one right person who matched him and his needs so perfectly, only to lose her again.

His eyes began to cloud with the sheen of wetness he'd seldom allowed. Searching frantically for something to take his mind off the pain, he spotted the gypsy's gift on the far corner of the desk. He reached out and picked up the heavy gold-and-ivory covered book, studying it.

He'd almost forgotten all about this. What nonsense it had been for the old woman to give him a book of fairy tales and tell him it would bring him to his destiny. Ridiculous.

But curiosity got the better of him as he turned the book in his hands. He couldn't remember ever actually reading any fairy tales before. But he did listen to a few told to him by his great-aunt Lucille. Now he wondered if his memories were the same as the real thing.

Opening the book and beginning to read, Nick absorbed each story. Remembered each plot. Relearned each lesson.

As he came to the story of Sleeping Beauty awakened by the kiss of her Prince Charming, exhaustion took over. His body was limp and his brain couldn't focus. He lowered his head to the desk and fell fast asleep. To dream about gypsies and witches, and beautiful sleeping princesses—all with Annie's face.

* * *

Passionata smiled down on the sleeping heir from far away. "Yes, let the magic take you, young Scoville. It is not a sleeping princess that has been awakened today, but a vulnerable and lonely prince.

"Wake up and take your destiny into your own hands. Your legacy has brought you to your heart's desire. Cherish it. Cherish her."

The gypsy waved a hand over her crystal ball and time spun forward.

Groggy and disoriented, Nick woke up several hours later. Something felt different in the room.

Suddenly he came alive. Something *was* very different. For the first time, Nick could see himself, his life and his mistakes with complete clarity. As clear as if it were one of the stories he'd read in the book.

Hell. He was the one that was different. Not the same selfish, controlling jerk who'd fallen asleep, laying on the gypsy's magic book. He shook his head in amazement.

It was a complete wonder that anyone could've stood for the man he used to be. He had turned into a bully— just like his father.

Christina popped into his mind. Poor, dear Christina. He'd badgered her into marrying him and then hounded her until she agreed to stay married after they discovered they couldn't have children. They hadn't loved each other and hadn't even been friends in the end.

The ache of remembering her woke him up to a new truth. He'd thought he was honoring her memory by not allowing pleasure into his life, by staying in his isolated and gray world and hiding from the desolation of not being able to father a child. But in fact, Christina would've hated that he'd done that in her name.

I'm sorry, Christina, he thought sadly. Sorry for everything. But I refuse to continue being a lost prince…

The book! The damn book must really be magic.

He looked around, half-expecting to see Annie and dying to tell her what he'd learned. But she wasn't there.

Oh, God, she was never going to be there again. The stabbing pain in his chest moved him. He had to find her, had to talk to her. Had to make her listen and understand. Tell her about the magic.

He started down the hall toward the pool house to wake her up. But he saw a light on under the door to the master suite, and changed directions instead.

When he opened the door, he saw her, pulling things out of a suitcase and putting them away in a drawer. Was he dreaming? Had he wanted her back so badly that his brain conjured her up?

"Annie?"

She turned her head, but there was no smile on her face for him. The vision must be real. If he'd dreamed her, she would've been laughing and happy to see him.

"Hello, Nick. You're up early. I was hoping to get this done before you needed to return to your room."

"Annie, what's going on?" He'd asked the question calmly, but then found himself holding his breath, waiting for the answer.

"I thought about it a lot and I've decided it was not very adult of me to walk away. I married you for better or worse and I have a child to consider." She shook her head sadly and dropped her hands to her side. "Even if we must live separate lives from a distance like your parents have always done, I intend to stay married and keep the promise I made."

It was as if a window opened to his soul. But Annie didn't understand. Somehow he would have to make her see.

He went to her side and gently turned her to face him. She kept her head down as if she couldn't bear to look at him. So he tenderly used his finger to lift her chin.

"Don't..." His voice faded and he swallowed hard, trying to sound steady when that was the very last thing he was feeling.

Finally, he tried again. "Don't stay with me out of duty, or because of our child. My mother did that and it ruined two lives, and nearly ruined several more."

Annie looked confused—and distant. He must make her understand that he'd changed. He fell to his knees before her and clasped both her hands in his own.

"Stay because if you go, you'll take the sun with you," he begged. "Stay because every day without you will put me back into a cold, gray hell. Stay because you make me more human..."

His voice hitched again and he had to swipe at his eyes to see her. "Stay because I love you, Annie. And I promise to never again make a decision alone."

"You love me?" Her voice was small, and her hands began to shake.

He was blinded by the wetness now and threw his arms around her body, pressing his face to her belly and the child they had made together. "I've never been in love before, my darling." His breath caught at saying the truth out loud.

"But I know I love you," he moaned. "You've got my loyalty, my heart, my soul…forever. Please don't turn me away. Make a real life with me."

Annie suddenly dropped to her knees and clung to him. "I don't know why or how you've changed. But I do know I love you so much. And I'll never leave as long as you just keep telling me you love me and keep on talking. We can make it. I know we can."

Nick kissed her, allowing every emotion he'd ever hidden to surge through his lips to hers. They *would* make it work.

Annie pulled back and smiled at him. "You know, I think I would love to marry you again. We'll have a big church wedding this time," she said with a chuckle. "And a *much* better honeymoon. I promise."

Nick dashed his hands across his eyes and bent to cover her laughing mouth with his own. What a fabulous life they would have together, laughing and sharing and making children.

He knew for certain now that their lives would end up being much more like a wonderful fairy tale than any daily reality could ever be. They gypsy's book had shown him the way.

Raising his eyes, he gave thanks to an unseen old gypsy woman and to the wonderful great aunt who'd been the reason he had been so gifted by love.

Because he knew their love came from the magic. It was his legacy.

Epilogue

The old gypsy woman, Passionata Chagari, picked up her heavy crystal and waited for the haze to clear. It was important that she see into young Scoville's future.

Everything must be as her father had directed. There could be no deviations from his wishes. Passionata had sworn on her life to deliver the proper legacies.

When the fog cleared from the crystal, a future day filled with brilliant sunshine on the ocean came into view. Sea and sky ran together in an indigo blue wash of color.

And through the choppy whitecaps appeared a double-masted sailing vessel, looking like a pirate ship with all her sails set and strained by the wind. Passionata smiled as she spotted the strawberry-blond crew, consisting of two strong and lean young men and two laughing and beautiful preteen girls. Their fresh young faces beamed with the promise of youth and good health.

They all worked together, following the orders of the captain and first mate. Their captain wore white slacks, a halter top and a navy blue cap pulled tightly down over her fiery red curls. She grinned over at the first mate as she tacked the tidy ship back and forth through the following seas and shouted over the winds to her crew.

First mate Nicholas Scoville's gold and silver hair blew across his eyes as he smiled contentedly upon his family and crew. Proud and so magically happy that he thought he might burst, Nick did as he did every day for the past eighteen years. He gave up silent thanks to an old gypsy and her father who, for reasons still unknown, had given him back his life—and left him with love.

From her vantage point through time, Passionata wished Nicholas Scoville well, nodding her head in approval. Her father could rest easy on that account. Another small part of the debt due to Lucille Steele had been repaid.

The old gypsy tilted the crystal once again, wanting to check on the rest of her charges. But the future clouded over in a gray mass, blinding her to the future for the next of Lucille's descendants.

Determined that nothing would stand in the way of the legacies, Passionata sat back and waited. The time and the vision for Tyson Steele would come. When it did, she was convinced all would be as ordained…and filled with magic.

* * * * *

HARLEQUIN® *Blaze*™

Three sisters whose power between
the sheets can make men feel better
than they ever have…literally!

Sexual Healing

Her magic touch makes those sheets sizzle

Join bestselling author Dorie Graham as
she tells the tales of women with ability
to heal through sex in

#196 THE MORNING AFTER
August 2005

#202 SO MANY MEN…
September 2005

#208 FAKING IT
October 2005

Be sure to catch this sensual miniseries
from Dorie Graham!

Look for these books at your favorite retail outlet.

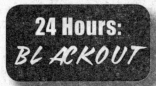

DYNASTIES: THE ASHTONS

continues in September with
CONDITION OF MARRIAGE
by Emilie Rose

Pregnant by one man, Mercedes Ashton enters
into a marriage of convenience with another
and finds that her in-name-only husband
ignites more passion than she ever imagined!

*Don't miss the drama as Dynasties: The Ashtons
unfolds each month, only in Silhouette Desire.*

Silhouette Desire

COMING NEXT MONTH

#1675 CONDITION OF MARRIAGE—Emilie Rose
Dynasties: The Ashtons
Abandoned by her lover, pregnant Mercedes Ashton turned to her good friend
Jared Maxwell for help. Jared offered her a marriage of convenience…that
soon flared into unexpected passion. But when the father of Mercedes's
unborn child returned, would her bond with Jared be enough to keep their
marriage together?

#1676 TANNER TIES—Peggy Moreland
The Tanners of Texas
Lauren Tanner was determined to get her life back on track…without the
assistance of her estranged family. When she hired quiet Luke Jordan, she
had no idea the scarred handyman was tied to the Tanners and prepared to use
any method necessary—even seduction—to bring Lauren back into the fold.

**#1677 STRICTLY CONFIDENTIAL ATTRACTION—
Brenda Jackson**
Texas Cattleman's Club: The Secret Diary
Although rancher Mark Hartman's relationship with his attractive secretary,
Alison Lind, had always been strictly professional, it changed when he was
forced to enlist her aid in caring for his infant niece. Now their business
arrangement was venturing into personal—and potentially dangerous—
territory.…

#1678 APACHE NIGHTS—Sheri WhiteFeather
Their attraction was undeniable. But neither police detective Joyce Riggs nor
skirting-the-edge-of-the-law Apache Kyle Prescott believed there could be
anything more than passion between them. They decided the answer to their
dilemma was a no-strings affair. That was their first mistake.

#1679 REFLECTED PLEASURES—Linda Conrad
The Gypsy Inheritance
Fashion model Merrill Davis-Ross wanted out of the spotlight and had
reinvented herself as the new plain-Jane assistant of billionaire Texan
Tyson Steele. But her mission to leave her past behind was challenged
when Tyson dared to look beyond Merrill's facade to find the real woman
underneath.

#1680 THE RICH STRANGER—Bronwyn Jameson
Princes of the Outback
When fate stranded Australian playboy Rafe Carlisle on her cattle station,
usually wary Cat McConnell knew she'd never met anyone like this rich
stranger. Because his wild and winning ways tempted her to say yes to night
after night of passion, to a temporary marriage—and even to having his baby!

SDCNM0805